A SEASON OF MAGIC

EVERGREEN HOLLOW CHRISTMAS BOOK FIVE

FIONA BAKER

JOIN MY NEWSLETTER

If you love beachy, feel-good women's fiction, sign up to receive my newsletter, where you'll get free books, exclusive bonus content, and info on my new releases and sales!

CHAPTER ONE

Margo Stoker had never pictured herself as a bride, and she could hardly believe her reflection as the bridal shop attendant who had been helping her that afternoon pinned a white veil into her hair in front of the mirror.

She'd ordered her dress a few months ago, from a small shop in Burlington that her mother, Rhonda Stoker, had recommended. Just thinking of the day that they'd all come to pick it out made her a little misty-eyed.

At first, she'd argued that she could just order some options online and try them on at home. She'd never been the type to imagine her wedding or daydream about what dress she would wear, and she was far more focused on the future where she'd be married to the love of her life, Dr. Spencer Thorpe, than she was on all the pageantry of the wedding itself. Her older sister, Caroline, had been sympathetic—she hadn't been all that excited to have a big wedding either, when she'd married her husband, Rhett. But Rhonda and Margo's other sister, Nora, who was an event planner, had firmly insisted that she needed to do the whole thing, and that she'd regret it one day if she didn't.

Which had led to all of the Stoker women and their children, a few months ago, piling into Lace and Thread to pick out Margo's wedding dress.

She had known right from the start that if she was going to have a wedding, it would be a Christmas wedding. She'd met Spencer during the holidays, after all, after she'd abruptly lost her job as a photojournalist at a magazine in New Jersey at the worst possible time of year for that to happen. That job loss had pushed her to go back home to Evergreen Hollow for the first time in years, and she'd met Spencer as a result. The holidays were special to them, and she'd known that a winter wedding was perfect for them. He'd agreed too, immediately.

The ladies had spent all afternoon that day looking at dresses, everything from satin ballgowns to delicate lace sheath dresses, and finally settled on the one that Margo was wearing as she looked in the mirror, astonished at how much she really looked like a bride.

It was a long, fitted gown with a high neck and long sleeves, all entirely made out of soft floral lace with a delicate eyelash fringe at the wrists and hem. She'd added a soft white fur stole that wrapped around her shoulders, and the delicate lace veil that the attendant had slipped into her hair was fringed with the same lace. She looked like a winter wonderland princess, and she clearly remembered Nora saying exactly that when she'd stepped out of the dressing room. That she looked like she was a fairy princess, out in the wintry woods with the snowy owls that she'd become obsessed with the winter before.

The dress was even more beautiful now that it had been altered to fit her perfectly. She slid her hands over the column of lace, admiring the way it outlined her figure, the way it looked classic and unique all at once. If she *had* dreamed of what she might look like as a bride, the dress she was wearing was exactly what she would have pictured.

"I can't believe I'm actually marrying Spencer,"

she said softly, glancing down at the sparkling tanzanite ring on her left hand.

That too was exactly what she would have imagined if she'd ever thought about what her engagement ring would one day look like. Spencer had picked out a ring that suited her perfectly, from the simple solitaire setting in white gold to the tanzanite stone from her favorite country that she'd ever visited.

And she'd traveled a lot.

For most of her life before the last two years, she'd globe-trotted constantly as a photojournalist. Her apartment in New Jersey had been more of a storage unit than a home, housing her clothes and the few pieces of IKEA furniture she owned.

She'd never stayed in one place for long, and she'd liked it that way. It had made her resistant to the idea of staying in a small town at first. Evergreen Hollow was ultimately her home, where she'd grown up—but it was also a place that she'd never planned to come back to for any length of time, if at all. She'd had her heart broken badly and had felt stifled there when she had been younger, and she had wanted her freedom.

She just hadn't expected it to be the place where her heart was put back together.

"Spencer isn't going to believe he's marrying *you*," Nora said from where she was sitting on one of the pink couches surrounding the three-way mirrors, bouncing little Madison on her lap. "You're the most gorgeous bride, Margo."

"It's just this place," Margo said, waving a hand. She'd ended up at Lace and Thread because all of the Stoker women had shopped for their wedding dresses there, from Rhonda to Nora and then Caroline—and now her. "They make beautiful brides."

"No, it's you too," Rhonda insisted, looking adoringly at her youngest daughter. "You are absolutely stunning. Spencer won't be able to take his eyes off of you."

"Can he ever?" Caroline joked, rocking her own baby, little Tobias. He was sleeping peacefully for now, clearly uninterested in the wedding enthusiasm all around him.

Margo couldn't help the smile on her face as she looked back at the mirror. The fact that her family was here with her for this moment meant so much to her. They, along with Spencer, were the reason she'd fallen in love with Evergreen Hollow again, why she was able to be happy there despite the slow pace and sameness of it all. Why she'd been able to look for ways to be fulfilled, even though she wasn't jetting off to a new country every other month.

She knew that Spencer was relieved that she'd settled in at last too. He'd been worried last Christmas, just before he proposed, that she wouldn't want to stay. That her restlessness after a year of living in Evergreen Hollow again meant that she wouldn't be able to handle it much longer. And she had to admit, she *had* been feeling restless. She had been struggling. And she hadn't wanted to let Spencer know just how true that was, because the last thing she ever wanted to do was hurt him, or make him feel like he wasn't enough.

Adventure had always been a part of her, a vital part of her personality. But she'd found new ways to fulfill that need, new things to occupy her so she didn't feel that wanderlust as intensely as she had before.

Last winter, she'd found those snowy owls that Nora had teased her about, and she'd convinced her boss, Sabrina, to let her do a two-page spread about them in the *Evergreen Hollow Gazette*. She'd searched out their nesting spots throughout the woods surrounding Evergreen Hollow, taken pictures, noted the best paths for tourists to hike and see them. And by the time the article had run in

January, she'd had a spread that had rivaled any of the projects she'd worked on for the magazine.

She'd been proud of herself for putting so much work into it and finding something to be passionate about at home, and her family and Spencer had been proud of her too.

Nora and Caroline had encouraged her to branch out too, to find more things that excited her and caught her interest. So she'd looked for those things, and she'd found them. Not only had she come up with more ideas for articles highlighting the variety of wildlife in the area, but she'd started teaching wildlife photography classes at the local community college a few nights a week.

That, more than anything else she'd done in the last two years, had made her feel like she'd finally found her niche. There were students of all ages in her classes, from actual college-age kids to middle-aged students who wanted to branch out into a new hobby, to elderly men and women who wanted to try something new in their golden years. She loved every part of it, from teaching them about the equipment to going out on photography field trips on the weekends, and it felt like she had found yet another fresh start.

Her eyes misted over as she looked in the mirror

again, glassy with tears of happiness. She could see her family behind her—her mother, and her two sisters, her little niece and nephew, and even Melanie Carter, who had always been Nora's friend but who she'd become close to in the last year too. It felt surreal that she was there with all of them, that she was going to get to marry the love of her life a week before Christmas, and she thought she'd never been happier.

"Is there anything else you want to alter or change?" the bridal shop attendant asked, and Margo glanced back at her family, waiting for their input.

"I don't think so," Rhonda said, misty-eyed as well with the same tears of happiness. Margo could see that Nora looked almost exactly the same, dabbing at the corners of her eyes as she bounced Madison. "The dress is perfect. You're a beautiful Christmas bride, Margo."

"I think we're good," Margo told the woman with a smile. "I'll go change out of it, and we can get it ready to come home with me?"

Twenty minutes later, she was back in her jeans and a thick, dark green woolen fisherman's sweater with a sheepskin-lined denim jacket over it. While the others waited, she paid the last installment on the dress as it was zipped into a pink garment bag with the shop name emblazoned on the front, and then they took it out to her car before all trooping across the road to one of the Stokers' favorite restaurants in Burlington.

It was a cozy English-style pub, with rustic tables set around a room that was warm from a crackling fireplace. The snow was thick outside, crunching under Margo's boots as they walked in. A pretty blonde hostess led them to a long table in between a window and the fireplace and they all sat down.

"I'll be right back with high chairs for the little ones," she said then hurried away as they all got settled.

"I can't believe our baby sister is getting married," Caroline said wistfully as she got Tobias situated, glancing at the menu out of the corner of her eye.

"I'm so excited." Nora grinned, doing the same with Madison as she handed her a soft-covered book to play with and passed around the rest of the menus that the server had left. "Out of all the events that I've planned, this one is definitely my favorite. And the most special to me."

"I feel a little guilty," Margo admitted as she sat down. "I wasn't there for either of your weddings. I was out of the country for work both times. I sent gifts, but I know that wasn't the same. And now you're putting so much into my wedding, it just doesn't feel fair."

It had been part of the reason she'd been so hesitant to do the full wedding, instead of just going to the courthouse with Spencer. She regretted missing her sisters' weddings, and she felt badly that they were so excited about hers.

"Nonsense," Rhonda said, just as Nora and Caroline both shook their heads. "The past is the past. There's no reason to let it spoil the now."

"Exactly," Nora said. "I'm just happy you let me do all the planning."

"I have *zero* opinions about flowers or place settings," Margo said with a laugh. "This wedding is going to be a million times better *because* you're the one planning it."

"Mom's right," Caroline adds. "It doesn't matter that you didn't make it to our weddings. You're home now. And we want this day to be the best possible celebration for you and our new brother-in-law."

Margo smiled, a warmth filling her chest at that. She'd wondered for a long time if she would ever really be able to go home if she wanted to, but she *had*. She'd come home, and there was no acrimony or resentment for the past, or how long she'd been gone. Everyone was just glad to have her here again.

She was lucky, she knew. She always had been.

Nora pulled out her event planner, tabbed with a few dozen colorful sticky tabs, and flipped it open so that she could show everyone what she'd been working on. Margo leaned over the table, looking at the fabric swatches that Nora was choosing between for tablecloths, trying to think of what she actually liked best as the server came back, and they all started to order their food—beginning with the warm squash dip that the restaurant was so famous for.

A little while later, as the air filled with the delicious fall scents of lamb stew and roasted chicken sandwiches, Margo looked around the table and knew once again that there was no chance she would ever want to leave again.

Evergreen Hollow was her home for good now.

And she had the best family that she could possibly ask for.

CHAPTER TWO

About halfway through his appointments for the day, Dr. Spencer Thorpe looked at his phone and hummed under his breath.

It was three in the afternoon, and he had enough appointments left that he had a feeling he wouldn't be leaving the clinic until at least eight. He was supposed to have dinner with Margo at The Mistletoe Inn that evening, but he knew he was going to have to text her and let her know he'd be late, or possibly not make it at all.

It had been like this for the last few months. Around the beginning of autumn, the small-practice medical clinic that had been established in the next town over for probably the last thirty years had closed its doors. The result of that closure was that

Spencer had become the next closest option, and most of the other practice's patients—especially the ones that liked the small-town feeling and didn't want to go to a major hospital—had ended up coming to him.

He was glad for the extra business, especially with the upcoming wedding, and he was even more glad to be able to help. It reaffirmed that he'd made the right decision, years ago, leaving San Francisco to come and work in Evergreen Hollow.

It felt good to be able to be there for those patients who needed someone familiar, to not have to shake up their routine too much other than driving a little bit further for their appointments.

But it had meant he'd been working a lot more, which had allowed him less time to see Margo lately. He missed spending time with her, especially this time of year when all of the memories from the very first part of their relationship seemed especially fresh. There were so many romantic winter activities that he wanted to do with her, and they just hadn't had the time.

Especially with the wedding right around the corner.

He'd been over the moon at the prospect of marrying her last year when he'd proposed, and he still was, but he'd definitely underestimated how much planning went into a wedding. Margo had wanted to elope, but he'd known there was no way her family would go for that, and he'd been right.

Truthfully, he was more than a little glad. She might not have been crazy about the idea of a big, traditional wedding, but he liked the idea. He was looking forward to a holiday celebration of their love in front of all of the most important people in their lives.

Fortunately, her sister Nora had stepped in to help plan the whole thing. He'd gotten to see firsthand why she'd been so sought after when she lived in Boston. She was an excellent event planner with a good eye, and she knew when to just make decisions and when to bring things to them for their input.

The parts that needed their input had kept them busy over the last several months though. They'd found the perfect venue, a gorgeous lodge in a snowy part of the hills surrounding Evergreen Hollow, where they could have the ceremony right in front of one of the most perfect views he'd ever seen.

Nora had come up with a number of mockups of rustic, charming invitations for them to choose from to send out, and he and Margo had spent several nights in front of the fire with mulled wine, trying to decide which one was perfect. They had decided on one with heavy, creamy stationery printed with cardinals interspersed with greenery, and their date nights after that had involved signing all the invitations before they could be sent out.

As much as the wedding planning had taken over their lives though, he wouldn't have changed it for anything. Rhonda and Donovan, his future in-laws, had mentioned a number of times that they would look back fondly on the chaos one day, and be glad they had those memories. And he believed them.

He smiled as he looked at the picture of Margo on his lock screen, sliding his thumb over it so he could text her and let her know that he was going to be late. It was his favorite picture of her, one that he'd snapped candidly while they were on a hike getting pictures for one of her articles. She was posing next to a nest with a few of the local birds sitting in it, sticking her tongue out because she'd seen him taking pictures of her. It was silly and lighthearted and fun, and those were all things that he thought of when he thought about his bride-to-be.

SPENCER: I'm sorry to tell you that I'm not going to make dinner tonight. I

still have patients, and I'm going to be here late. Raincheck???

MARGO: I can cover a plate for you. Come over after? I'll be up for a while. Mom made gingerbread cookies.

SPENCER: You know I can't resist gingerbread cookies. Or you. I'll be there as soon as I can.

He smiled as he sent the last text, knowing it was true. He knew he was going to want to go home and fall directly into bed after what had been a series of very long days, but he also couldn't turn down an opportunity to spend time with Margo, especially not when she asked him to come over so sweetly. He missed her, even when they hadn't been apart for that long, which he thought was a good sign for their marriage. He never felt like he could spend enough time with her, and he didn't think he ever would.

The nurse came to the door of the exam room, opening it and ushering in Leon Woodrow, who Spencer knew well. He owned the Sugar Maple General Store in town, and Spencer had liked him from the moment they'd met.

"How are you feeling?" he asked as Leon came in. "That flu that's been going through town is a pretty unpleasant bug."

The older man sat down on the exam table, running one hand through his gray hair. "It definitely is," Leon agreed. "But I'm feeling fine now."

"Well, we'll just do a quick check-up," Spencer said. "Just to make sure you're all healthy now."

"How are the wedding plans going?" Leon asked with a grin as Spencer looked over his chart, and Spencer chuckled.

"Busy, as expected. But we're both so excited. And it's extra special that Nora is helping us with the planning. Seeing it all come together is really amazing."

"She's something else," Leon agreed. "Those three girls together are a force of nature. And you got the wildest one," he added humorously. "It's nice to see Margo settling down after traveling for so long. We all thought she'd never come home to roost for good. It's nice to see that she's happy back home."

"She is," Spencer said confidently. "And she's really coming into her own here. I know she's excited to start a new chapter."

Leon's words lingered with him though, as he finished the exam and let the older man know that he was doing great, before moving on to his next patient. He'd worried, last holiday season, that Margo seemed restless and unsettled. Since the very beginning of their relationship, he'd been unsure if someone with her adventurous spirit would be able to settle down for long. Spencer himself had lived in a big city for a long time, and he was well aware of how different Evergreen Hollow was from a place like that. He also knew that since last Christmas, Margo had found ways to create exciting new projects for herself at her job, balancing her desire for adventure with her love of the town where she had grown up.

This new phase of life would be an adjustment for them both. Settling down for good, moving in together, starting a family—those were some of the biggest milestones two people could go through.

Still, he believed with all his heart that they were ready for those milestones. That when she said her vows and made her commitment to him, she would mean it absolutely.

And so would he.

Around nine-thirty that evening, Caroline settled into a chair at her kitchen table, completely exhausted. She'd just finished putting Toby down to sleep, and cleaned the entire kitchen from top to bottom after making a dinner of pot roast and vegetables that would give them leftovers for a few days.

Now she just had to tidy up the living room, and she could go to bed and try to get a little bit of reading in. She'd gotten a new book from the library, a historical epic that she'd been wanting to read, but she'd barely gotten a few pages in. It felt like every few paragraphs, she had to go back and reread because her mind felt so foggy. And she fell asleep within a few pages anyway.

Letting out a soft breath, she tucked a piece of hair that had fallen loose from her ponytail behind her ear and pushed up the sleeves of her flannel shirt that had slid down.

She had to admit that taking care of two houses and a family was a lot. For all of her adult life, she'd been helping her parents, Rhonda and Donovan, run The Mistletoe Inn. And she'd always loved it. It was the family business, her parents' pride and joy, and hers. She'd never regretted for a second devoting her life to helping them run it, and for years and years, it had been her whole life.

But then, she'd married Rhett a few years ago, and become a stepmother to his now pre-teen son, Jay. Things had started getting more chaotic then, when she'd no longer lived upstairs at the inn, but had moved out to a small cottage further back on the property that her parents had deeded to her and Rhett as a wedding gift.

Juggling the needs of helping to run a bed-and-breakfast along with the needs of her husband and stepson had been difficult, but manageable. And then last Christmas, she'd unexpectedly gotten pregnant, and everything had gotten so much more difficult.

The pregnancy had come out of nowhere, but she'd been happy about it. So had Rhett, who had been absolutely overjoyed to expand their little family. She'd been even more tired then, struggling to manage it all, but she'd written it off as just being pregnant, and expected that after the baby arrived, she'd go back to her old capable self.

She'd always handled everything just fine, juggling a dozen plates and never dropping any of them, and she saw no reason why that needed to change, even though Nora had warned her that it would.

Nora had been right, she thought absently as she rubbed her temples and looked out to the still-messy living room. It felt like there were never enough hours in the day now. Running a small family business was like a child all on its own, and she had her own house, her stepson, and now little Toby. He was a good baby, but she was still beyond tired, and it didn't feel like that was letting up anytime soon.

She heard the front door open, and the familiar tread of her husband's heavy work boots on the entryway floor. Rhett was back from his shift at the fire department, and she was so glad that he was home. If she'd been less tired, she would have jumped up and run across the house to give him a hug.

A few minutes later, he padded into the kitchen. She saw the wrinkle of concern on his forehead as soon as he saw her sitting there, and he leaned down to give her a quick kiss, giving her an appraising look as he pulled back.

"You look exhausted," he said, giving her another kiss on the top of her head. "Can I get you something? Some apple cider, maybe?"

Caroline cracked a smile at that.

"You absolutely can," she said tiredly. "If you'll put some whiskey in it."

Rhett grinned. "I can do that. Where's Jay?" he asked as he went to the upper cupboard where they kept their alcohol, taking down a bottle of Kentucky bourbon and heading to get the jug of the fresh-pressed apple cider they'd bought out of the refrigerator. "Also, do you want this hot or cold?"

"Hot sounds amazing." Caroline leaned back in her chair, stifling a yawn. "Jay is upstairs doing his homework in his room. I was going to go up and check on him after I finished cleaning up the living room."

Rhett shook his head, pouring apple cider and whiskey into a small pot with a cinnamon stick and turning on the stove.

"I'll go check on our son," he said, stirring the cider until it was warm then pouring it into a mug. "You drink this." He set it on the table next to her elbow. "And then I'll leave the living room to you, since you're so particular about how you like it," he added with a grin and a wink, giving her a quick peck on the cheek.

Caroline let out a soft breath as she watched him leave the room, picking up the warm mug of cider and cradling it in her hands.

It was perfect, she thought as she took a drink, fresh and crisp with just the right amount of cinnamon and the light, spicy burn of the whiskey. She could feel her muscles relaxing with every sip, and she glanced around the kitchen, taking in the familiar, cozy sight.

She loved the inn. She loved what her parents had built, and what she'd helped them keep going over the years. She loved her husband, and her family, and the life they shared. She loved Evergreen Hollow, and the home that she'd always made in it.

Everything in her life was perfect.

So why am I so tired?

She grinned wryly at the thought as she surveyed her surroundings again, trying to work up the energy to get up and head into the living room to do her final tidying up for the evening.

Another yawn tugged at her lips, and she put a hand over her mouth, shaking her head in bemusement. There had always been plenty of things in her life to keep her busy, but it hadn't always felt like *so much*.

There had been times, before Nora and Margo had come home, when Caroline had felt like she had to do everything on her own. But she'd always felt like she could take care of all of it, and even in the busiest and most stressful of times, she'd been confident that she wouldn't be overwhelmed.

But she knew from years of experience just how crazy the holiday season could get, how busy and chaotic. Last Christmas, there had been the unexpected addition of her realization that she was pregnant, which had definitely added to the whirlwind feeling of the holiday season. And now they had a three-month-old baby. Although Rhett was an amazing father and was great about helping out with Tobias, Caroline definitely felt like she was struggling more than she ever had before when it came to keeping everything running smoothly these days.

As she took one last sip of her cider before getting up and heading into the living room, it struck her suddenly just how much had changed since she had met and fallen in love with Rhett. Her life was immeasurably better with him in it, as well as their children. She adored Jay, and Tobias had brought so much light and happiness to their lives.

But now that she had a family of her own, maybe she needed to change the way she looked at things. She'd always been the type of person to insist that she could do it all, but with all of the new responsibilities and complexities that had entered her life, she was starting to wonder if that was true anymore.

Maybe it was time to look for ways to take a few things off her plate.

CHAPTER THREE

"What do you think of your new sweater?" Nora held it up as she scooped Madison up with her other arm, swinging her back and forth as she plopped her onto the changing table and tugged the soft red sweater over her head. Madison looked adorable, in a pair of black leggings and the red sweater with a knitted reindeer on the front, complete with a little bobble attached to it for the nose. She had a headband for her too, in a red cable-knit pattern, and she slipped it into Madison's dark hair as the little girl babbled and cooed.

She'd been looking forward to this morning. The wedding planning was coming down to the wire now, and it was time for all of the little finishing touches that were some of her favorite parts of all of this. She and Madison were headed to the Sugar Maple General Store to get some of the odds and ends that she needed for those finishing touches, and she couldn't wait to pick them out.

Madison grabbed a handful of her sweater, a red Angora top that she'd paired with her favorite dark jeans to subtly match her daughter today. Nora gently pried herself loose, holding Madison's small hands in hers as she swayed back and forth, cooing at her daughter in return.

She adored being a mother. At first, in the very early days, she could admit that she'd struggled at times. Madison had had trouble sleeping, leaving both her and Aiden chronically exhausted and wondering when they'd get another full night's sleep.

But Aiden was such a wonderful father that in the end, it hadn't been as hard as it might have been otherwise. Aiden had always been there for her through all of those early struggles, trading out with her when it was time to get up and feed Madison or check on her as she cried throughout the night, and finding whatever opportunities he could to take things off of her plate. Even though he worked more than full-time sometimes, running his carpentry business, he'd always stepped in and found ways to give her time to rest and recover.

Neither of them had had any experience with being parents before, and the whole experience of learning it together had brought them closer together, instead of pushing them apart. They'd both found peace during those difficult early days in knowing that they'd look back on those memories eventually, stronger together and more in love because of it, remembering how they'd started building their little family.

A knock at the door downstairs jolted her out of her reverie, and she swept Madison up off of the changing table, putting her on her hip as she headed downstairs. She'd decorated for Christmas the day after Thanksgiving, and the banister of the stairs was wrapped in festive greenery, interspersed with small red velvet and red plaid bows. She'd put a red runner all the way down too, leading into the foyer that was bracketed with more greenery, and smelled wonderfully of the cinnamon-scented broom that was hung above the door.

Margo walked in a second later, dusting snow off of her boots. "It smells so *good* in here," she remarked as she took her boots off and followed Nora into the main area of the house, as Nora gathered up the last things she needed for the trek into town. "And it's so *clean!*" She put her hands on her hips, surveying both Nora and Madison as Nora tucked a few small packets of fruit snacks into Madison's bag. "And the matching outfits—" She grinned. "You're really rocking this whole mom thing."

"Thanks," Nora said with a laugh. "It took us some time to get here, honestly. Took some practice, but we've hit our stride. Haven't we?" she cooed at Madison, tickling one palm as Madison tried to grab for the last packet of fruit snacks. "Things have become much more orderly in the Masters household recently," she added. "It really is all going great. I'm really happy. We all are."

"Good." Margo grinned at her niece as Nora and Madison walked by, taking the baby for a minute as Nora handed her over so that Nora could get her coat and boots on. "Do you want to take your car or mine?"

"We can take mine," Nora offered. "It's newer, I know your old Subaru has held out all these years, but the car seat and stuff are already in mine too."

She'd given in last year, when Madison was born, and bought something bigger than her Toyota that she'd driven back when she lived in Boston. The Stoker family swore by their Subarus, and she'd picked out a newer Outback, complete with heated leather seats that she was in love with. Margo and

Caroline both had older, more rustic models, but she'd gotten one in a gorgeous red color, with sleek beige seats inside, as glamorous as a car designed to trek through snow and ice could possibly be.

The whole family had agreed that it suited her. Nora had left a good bit of her designer habits behind after moving back to Evergreen Hollow, but she still liked dressing up and having a bit of glam in her life, something that she'd gotten from her mother. Caroline took more after their father, and Margo fell somewhere in the middle.

"My seat heaters gave out last winter and I still haven't gotten them fixed," Margo said with a sigh. "With all the wedding craziness, I haven't had time to go to the shop, and when I do have time, I keep forgetting. So yeah, that's actually better."

"That's *definitely* better." Nora scooped Madison back out of Margo's arms, and carried her out to the car, buckling her in the back as it warmed up. In no time at all, they were on the road, cruising to Main Street where they could stop for coffee before going to Sugar Maple.

Once upon a time, Nora had thought she'd never be able to live outside of Boston again, with its endless options, myriad stores, and dozens of restaurants. But she'd found that once she adjusted, there was something comforting and warm about the idea that she could go to the same place, and pick out her favorite coffee in the morning, and always feel like it was another place to come home to. It didn't hurt, of course, that The Mellow Mug was also run by her best friend since they were children, Melanie.

"Doing some wedding planning?" Melanie asked as Nora and Margo walked in, and Margo nodded.

"Picking up some last-minute items. We're really getting into the planning weeds now, but Nora loves it."

"I do," Nora confirmed, peering at the pastries through their glass case. "I definitely think I want a piece of that pumpkin loaf to go. And a cinnamon latte. Extra hot."

"Coming right up. You want a maple pumpkin latte?" Melanie looked at Margo with a grin, and Margo pursed her lips.

"I think I'll do a white chocolate peppermint mocha, actually." Margo said. "And a chocolate croissant?"

"Delicious." Melanie took Nora's card as she handed it over, waving off Margo's attempts to pay.

"You're not even letting me pay you for planning my wedding," Margo complained. "You could at least let me buy you coffee."

"Nope." Nora shook her head. "Not a chance. This is fun for me. I wouldn't let you pay me no matter how hard you tried. Anyway, I planned Caroline's too. This is my wedding gift to you."

"Fine," Margo conceded with a grin. "And it's the best possible gift you could have given me."

A few minutes later, coffee in hand, the two women walked down the street to the Sugar Maple General Store. Nora set Madison in the rocking chair next to the counter with her stuffed reindeer toy, while she and Margo browsed the shelves looking for the perfect wedding favors for the guests.

"What about these?" Nora held up two tiny jars of homemade jelly, wrapped in a tiny ribbon around each. "These are adorable."

"Oh, they *are*." Margo looked closer. "We could do the apple jelly and pumpkin butter. And this." She pointed to a display that had small candles wrapped in burlap. "There's fir, and there's also this one. Honey bourbon. It smells so good." She bent down, breathing them in. "One of each, maybe?"

"I can't think of a wedding favor I would rather get than jam and candles," Nora said with a laugh. "Much better than those little bags of almonds. Oh! And this."

She pointed out a basket that had handmade

goat's milk soap, infused with various herbs. One had small bits of chamomile flower, and another had sprigs of rosemary, peeking out of the creamy surface.

"Pretty soap is definitely a winner!" she declared. "I would never use it, it's too pretty. But I'd definitely look at it in my bathroom."

"I'd use it," Margo declared, picking up the rosemary bar and sniffing it. "Oh, this is perfect too. Okay, so how are we going to arrange them?"

"These." Nora led Margo over to a shelf at the back of the shop, where there was a display of small wooden boxes that Aiden had made over the winter last year, and that Leon had stocked at the shop on consignment. "Aiden carved these. A little personal touch. We'll put two jams, a soap, and two candles in each little box, and put it at each guest's place setting."

"And I'll give you a discount for buying in bulk!" Leon called out from across the shop, making Margo laugh.

"I love it," she said firmly. "That's the best idea, Nora. It's just right for the kind of wedding we're having."

"That's why they used to pay me the big bucks." Nora grinned, getting a basket to start carrying the

items to the counter for Leon to ring up and
package.

"Bethany was just saying to me the other day
how perfect these little jars would be for some kind
of favor." Leon held up one of the small jars of
pumpkin butter between his fingers. "She's going to
get a real kick out of this."

"Yeah, I think so too," Nora agreed.

"Say," he added, as he began to wrap the more
delicate items in paper and slip them into bags, "who
did you end up getting to photograph the wedding? I
know you've always been real into photography and
such."

"I—" Margo stopped, cocking her head slightly,
as if she'd been completely caught off guard.

"Oh my gosh, you haven't thought about it, have
you?" Nora asked, her eyes widening. "And *I* didn't
think about asking you yet. I should have had that
checked off weeks ago."

"Even being a photographer, *I* didn't think about
it," Margo said, laughing. "That's such a huge thing, I
can't believe I let that slip. But I think I might have
an idea."

"What?" Nora scooped Madison up out of the
rocking chair, setting her on her hip as Leon finished
packaging up the last of the favors. "Because it's

going to be hard to find anyone who still has that weekend open so close to the date."

"What if we put a disposable camera on each person's seat?" Margo suggested. "The truth is, I think I was putting off finding a photographer for so long that I forgot about it, because it's the most stressful pick for me. I'm a photographer myself, so anyone who does it professionally, I'm going to nitpick their work to death. But if I'm *not* getting professional photos, if they're just all the candid photos that the people Spencer and I love have gotten of us all day, then all I'll see is how much they care about us, and what parts of our day they thought were important to document. It won't matter if they're technically 'good' or not, because that's not the point of them."

"That's a really great idea," Nora said, a smile spreading across her face. "I honestly don't know why we didn't think of that sooner."

"That sounds like a good way to make some wonderful memories," Leon agreed. "You'll really treasure those."

"I know Mom would love to help you turn them into a scrapbook after the wedding too," Nora added. "Let's grab some disposable cameras, then, and we'll add them to the haul for today."

They had just finished adding the disposable cameras to the small pile of things that Leon needed to ring up, when the door that separated the general store from the grooming salon next door—which Leon's wife, Bethany, owned—swung open. A small, barking cloud of fur came barreling out down the aisle next to where Nora and Margo were standing.

"Oh look at *you!*" Margo cried out, kneeling down as the small dog came running toward them. But the tiny animal ran straight for Madison instead, who was sitting in the rocking chair once again while Nora and Margo looked for the cameras.

She let out a squeal, lunging forward before either Nora or Margo could grab her, reaching for two big handfuls of the puppy's floppy ears. Nora gasped, looking up as Bethany came running down the aisle as well, slightly out of breath.

"That's a very friendly puppy," Nora remarked as she leaned down and scooped Madison up away from the puppy, relieved that it hadn't bitten her when she'd grabbed it. "Its owners must really give it a lot of affection. It looks like it can't wait to see them again."

Bethany sighed, reaching down to scoop the dog up. At eye-level, wriggling in Bethany's arms, Nora could see that it looked like a mixture of a King

Charles Spaniel, and maybe something slightly fluffier. The puppy was adorable, with white fur speckled in brown, and long floppy ears that were mostly brown, along with a happily wagging tail that was the same.

"I actually found her in the alley outside," Bethany explained, scratching the puppy behind her ears. "She was all by herself. I brought her in and cleaned her up. She's been super friendly the whole time, one of the easiest dogs I've ever groomed. Usually they can be difficult, especially with as many tangles as this one had, but she was sweet all through it."

"Aww." Margo leaned forward and scratched the puppy behind her ears, and Madison craned to get out of Nora's arms, reaching for the dog again.

"That's not our puppy," Nora told her daughter, bouncing her in her arms as she reached for the bags that Leon had waiting. "I hope you find her owners soon," she added, looking sympathetically at the small dog and then at Bethany. "She's too cute to be on her own."

"I agree," Bethany said. "I'm sure someone will turn up soon."

"I hope so. Margo, are you ready?" Nora glanced over at Margo, who reluctantly gave up petting the dog as they both headed back out to the car with their shopping haul.

"I can't believe anyone would abandon a dog so cute," Margo lamented as they walked out. "She must have owners somewhere."

"I'm sure she does," Nora said firmly, sliding into the driver's seat. "And Bethany will figure it out. Meanwhile, we have a wedding to finish planning." She handed Margo a magazine that she'd tabbed a few pages in, hoping for some input, and Margo flipped through it as they drove back to the inn.

By the time they got back, where Rhonda had a lunch of cranberry turkey and gravy sandwiches waiting for them, Nora had forgotten all about the puppy.

CHAPTER FOUR

Early Saturday morning, Margo was just finishing getting ready to head out for her wildlife photography class when she heard Rhonda downstairs, calling for her. She hurried down the stairs, grabbing her coat and scarf as she went.

"I have to be at class in forty-five minutes," she said breathlessly. "What's up? The teacher can't be late."

"I think the teacher is the only one who *is* allowed to be late," Rhonda said with a laugh. "Anyway, I won't hold you up. You just had a package delivered, that's all."

Margo's eyes widened as Rhonda handed over the small box to her, and she saw the return address. "Oh!" she exclaimed, looking toward the kitchen. "Where's Caroline? I want to show her too."

"What about me?" Caroline walked out from the entry room, still holding the guest log. "What's going on?"

"Margo got a package," Rhonda explained. "She wanted to show us what it was."

"I was just about to grab some coffee. I'll bring us all some," Caroline said, hurrying past into the kitchen as Margo sat down on the couch in front of the fireplace. Rhonda sank down next to her, peering at the box.

Caroline emerged a moment later with three mugs of coffee, topped with whipped cream and small sprinkles of crushed peppermint candy. "Here you go," she said, setting them all down, and Margo laughed.

"Thank you," she said, reaching for it to take a sip. "I'm going to have to run in just a few minutes though, seriously. I have class."

"Which just means you need more caffeine," Caroline said, taking a sip of her coffee. "Mom crushed the candies this morning for peppermint mochas, so I couldn't let that go, not when I know how much you like them."

"How much caffeine have you had already?"

Margo asked teasingly. "You look a little tired, honestly." She frowned, her expression turning to concern, and Caroline just shrugged.

"The to-do list never seems to end," she admitted. "Especially with a new baby. But that's just how the holidays go, you know?"

"Like last year, when you and Rhett were both so busy that you got away with not telling him you were pregnant for *weeks*?" Margo teased, and Caroline nodded.

"Exactly. The holidays are always insane. I'm sure it will all feel more manageable once they're past. And I didn't sleep well last night either. So that's part of it."

Margo nodded, taking another drink of her coffee before she started to open up the package at Rhonda's urging. She tore off the tape, carefully slipping one end open before pulling out two small, identical blue velvet boxes and setting them on the coffee table.

"Your wedding rings!" Rhonda exclaimed, and she gasped as Margo opened the first box.

Hers was the first one, a thin white gold band with small diamonds set into the gold, so they couldn't easily be knocked loose. Spencer's was in the box next to it, a wider, smooth white gold band.

They were perfect, exactly what she and Spencer had picked out together.

"Those are beautiful!" Caroline exclaimed, setting down her mug of coffee to lean in and get a closer look, along with Rhonda. "They suit you both perfectly."

"I thought so," Margo said, looking at them both again before she gently set the boxes down. "Spencer wanted something very simple, since he's at the clinic all day, working with patients. And I can't be trusted with anything too flashy, I'll knock it loose in no time. So this was just the right amount of sparkle."

Rhonda reached down, squeezing Margo's hand as she beamed at her, a mist of tears in her eyes. "I can't wait for your wedding day," she said with a smile. "You found such a wonderful man. All three of my girls found wonderful men. And now I get to see my youngest get married too. I couldn't ask for anything more, honestly."

"Nora is doing such an incredible job with the planning too," Margo said enthusiastically. "I don't think I could do it without her."

"She was the reason mine went off without a hitch," Caroline said. "I couldn't begin to think of what I wanted. I hadn't ever really imagined what kind of wedding I would have either," she added, picking up her coffee for another sip. "She just *pictures* it. It's a really amazing talent."

"It is," Rhonda agreed, picking up one of the rings to look more closely at it again.

Margo looked down at her left hand as Rhonda and Caroline passed the rings back and forth, finishing her coffee. As always, she felt a small flutter of happiness, looking down at the purple-green stone in the white-gold setting. The ring meant so much to her, because he'd picked out something that was so specifically perfect for her. He'd paid attention, and that meant everything.

The ring signified their new life together in Evergreen Hollow, the one that he'd asked her to spend with him, but it was so much more than that too. It showed that he understood and loved her adventurous spirit, because he'd chosen a stone from her favorite place in the world that she'd visited. It showed that he knew that she was spontaneous and quick to do things on the spur of the moment, because he'd chosen something simple and sturdy that could last no matter what.

Something that would last through thick and thin, just like them.

"Spencer knows you so well," Rhonda said, echoing Margo's thoughts as she set the ring boxes back down. "I still love the engagement ring he picked for you."

"Me too." Margo smiled, slipping the wedding band free of the box to try it on with her engagement ring, to show Rhonda and Caroline. It fit snugly up against the other white gold band, sparkling in the sunlight. "He's perfect. And even though he's more of a homebody, he's really embraced the things I love to do too. He's gotten used to me going on hikes, and doesn't worry so much, even though he knows I can be prone to accidents sometimes."

"Twice in two years," Caroline cut in with a smirk. "*Very* prone."

Margo laughed. "You're not wrong," she admitted, thinking of how she'd broken her leg right after coming back to Evergreen Hollow, and then last Christmas, twisted her wrist while looking for snowy owls for an article. "But now he just says it's lucky that I'm marrying a doctor if I'm going to go do things like that. And he's been so supportive of the photography classes that I'm teaching. It takes up half of my Saturdays, when we could be doing things together, but he knows it's important to me to keep busy and find ways to do the things I love in new and interesting ways. And we're going to the *Galapagos* for our honeymoon."

"Wow." Caroline's eyebrows rose. "That's very adventurous. I'm impressed, honestly. I wouldn't have thought Spencer would be that adventurous."

"He was nervous at first, but he's willing to go for me. It's not his preferred trip, but he's excited to share something that I love, and see the kind of place that I used to go to all the time. And I promised that we'd go somewhere less exotic, like Ireland, for our first wedding anniversary," Margo added with a laugh. "But that's the thing! He compromises, and he always insists on compromising with the things that he knows are important to me. It means a lot, because I'd be willing to do it the other way around. But he *wants* to try all of the new things I want to show him first. And it really shows that he loves me."

"Showing love is the most important thing in a marriage," Rhonda agreed firmly. "You can say the words all you want, but it's the actions that really matter. When you see how much they love you day in and day out, you don't ever doubt it."

"I feel the same way about Rhett." Caroline smiled, and the tired lines around her eyes softened. "He always shows me, even when he's busy or tired. It's amazing, really."

"That's why I want to do something special." Margo set the bands side by side on the table again, considering. "I want Spencer to know just how ready I really am to settle down in Evergreen Hollow and be his wife. I know he has worried in the past, and he's had reason to. I've been fidgety and uncertain, and I've struggled to fit back in here. But I've found where I fit, and I want him to know that I'm all in now, forever."

"I think he knows," Rhonda said with a smile. "But I think he'll love anything that you might want to do for him."

"What if I get the rings specially engraved?" Margo picked them up, looking at the width. "I think there's enough room on each of them. It would be a symbol that shows Spencer I'm his forever, right there on our rings, where we can always see it."

Rhonda smiled. "I think that's a beautiful idea."

"I like it too," Caroline agreed. "What would you put on there?"

"Well..." Margo thought for a moment. "I didn't think Evergreen Hollow would be my home again until I came back and met Spencer. What about 'my heart has found its home'?"

"I love that—" Rhonda started to say, just as they heard the shuffling of boots in the entryway kicking off snow, and Spencer's voice calling out from the front door.

"Hi there! Rhonda?"

"Oh no." Margo flushed pink, hurriedly grabbing the rings and closing the small velvet boxes, pushing them back into the larger box they'd come in. "Look natural," she hissed as she tucked the box behind her, straightening up and grabbing her coffee mug.

The other two women did the same, but as Spencer walked into the living room, Margo could see his eyebrows raise as he looked at the three of them. There was a suspicious look on his face as if he could clearly tell that something was up, and Margo tried to look innocent as she scooted back further on the couch to hide the rings.

Spencer walked over to the couch, leaning down to drop a kiss on Margo's cheek. She leaned back as he did, distracting him from possibly seeing the box by twisting around and giving him a kiss full on the lips.

"I'm surprised to see you here," he said with a smile. "I thought you'd already be on your way to class."

"I was. But I wanted to stop by and see Mom and Caroline. Caroline got me coffee, so..." She trailed off, holding up the mug, and Spencer's smile broadened into a grin.

"Exactly why I came by. I know it's the time of

year when Mrs. Stoker's delicious peppermint mochas make an appearance, and I was hoping that I could swing by and convince her to give me one to go." Spencer looked innocently at his future mother-in-law. "I have some work to get done at the clinic, so I thought I'd pop by while I was out, on my way."

"And a breakfast burrito?" Rhonda teased him, and Margo flushed, remembering the breakfast her mother had conned him into staying longer at the inn with, long ago when she and Spencer had first met, and she'd been convinced nothing could keep her in Evergreen Hollow.

"I would never say no," Spencer said hopefully, and Rhonda laughed as she stood.

"I'm all out of burrito fixings, but I have pumpkin cinnamon muffins. I'll grab you one of those and a coffee to go," she told him with a smile.

Margo leaned up against the couch, kissing him again. "You ran out of coffee, didn't you?" she asked teasingly, and Spencer nodded.

"I did. I'll have to go by the store on my way home from the clinic this afternoon."

"I can pick some up after class." Margo tilted her head back against the back of the sofa, looking up at him. "Pretty soon you'll have me to help keep house anyway. And then you'll never run out of coffee again."

Spencer chuckled, coming around the couch to sit next to her. "You forget things from the store even when you have a list in your hand," he teased her, and Caroline laughed from the armchair.

"That's true," she said. "I stopped asking Margo to run grocery errands pretty quickly after she moved back into the inn."

"Okay, fine." Margo laughed, finishing her coffee. "I'll admit my very *transient* lifestyle up to this point didn't exactly teach me homemaking skills. But I'll just have to work on it."

Spencer leaned over, giving her a kiss on the temple. "I love you even if you do forget groceries," he told her firmly. "I'm not marrying you for your domestic skills anyway. I'm marrying you because you're my best friend."

"Oh, Spencer." Margo let out a sigh, leaning into him as Caroline laughed, taking both her and Margo's empty coffee mugs and leaving the couple alone for a moment, while Rhonda finished getting the coffee together for Spencer. "I can't wait for our wedding."

"Me too." He gave her another hug. "You're going to be late for class."

"I know." She stood up, hurriedly managing to sweep the box into her coat pocket without Spencer noticing. "I'll see you tonight for date night."

"Sounds good." He gave her another quick kiss, and then she hurried toward the door, looking at her watch. She was running short on time, but she thought she might be able to swing by Sugar Maple on her way and drop the rings off with Leon to have them engraved.

She was determined to be the best wife that Spencer could possibly ask for. Their sweet, unexpected conversation had just made her feel that much more strongly about it, and she couldn't wait to get started.

More than anything, she couldn't wait to show him that, with the surprise of the engraved rings.

CHAPTER FIVE

Later that day, back at her own cottage, Caroline ran through her mental to-do list once again.

Toby was playing happily in his playpen, gurgling to himself as he tossed around a set of large, connected plastic rings. She glanced over at him, smiling, and then looked at the clock. Jay would be home from school soon, and she still had a lot more things to do than she had hours in the day. Not the least of which was the fact that she needed to get dinner started.

She'd spent all day running around after Margo had left. She'd enjoyed the small coffee break with her mother and her sister, but it had left her thirty minutes behind in an already packed schedule.

The inn was at capacity for the weekend, which

meant housekeeping for every room, and making sure that all of the guests had anything special that they'd asked for. She had notes for every guest, their likes and dislikes, if they'd bought additional packages or just had recurring requests from prior visits, but she'd had to go over them multiple times this morning, feeling over and over like she'd forgotten something.

Then there was helping her mother with meal prep, and helping her father with the chickens and goats, and office paperwork, as well as finding out if there were any repairs around the inn that needed to be made, and all of the little things that always managed to find a way to add themselves to her to-do list.

She glanced over at Toby again, the sight of him sorting through blocks now in the center of his playpen making her smile, and set about getting dinner ready. She had all the ingredients for her favorite winter casserole, involving butternut squash, sage, ham, potatoes, and heavy cream.

She put on some soft background Christmas music in the kitchen as she worked, humming to herself and letting herself unwind just a little. She'd gotten much better at cooking over the years, and now it felt a bit meditative, something that she could just focus directly on and cut out all the noise of the endless other things that needed doing.

Other things that, once the casserole was finished, she could focus on.

She slid the casserole dish into the oven, set a timer, and walked into the living room where Toby was still happily playing. There was plenty that needed doing in that room alone—she needed to vacuum, dust, and finish putting up the Christmas decorations that were still sitting in their plastic tote next to the fireplace.

The tree was up and decorated, but she had mantle decorations and things for the stairs and the rest of the house to arrange. But, she thought as she looked around, she could sit down for a minute. Just a minute, and close her eyes, while she listened to Toby's happy babbling and the soft sound of the wind blowing the snow around outside.

Before she knew it, she suddenly heard the sound of Rhett's boots kicking off snow in the entryway, and the door opening as he walked into the house. She jolted up, realizing with a start that she must have fallen asleep.

"Do you have something in the oven?" Rhett called out from the entryway, and Caroline jumped up, the acrid scent hitting her nose a second after he said it.

"Dinner's burning!" she gasped, rushing to the kitchen. She yanked open the oven, pulled out the smoking casserole dish and dropped it on top of the stove. One look at it told her that it was unsalvageable; she must have fallen asleep so hard that she hadn't even heard the timer go off. It was completely burnt to a crisp.

She was going to have to start all over again from scratch. The thought hit her so hard that she started to cry, looking at the mess of dinner in front of her. She was far too overwhelmed.

Rhett's arms slipped around her waist from behind, and she felt him squeeze her gently as he rested his chin on her shoulder. "It's okay," he said calmly. "But it's probably a good thing that you're married to a fireman."

That made Caroline laugh through her tears, sniffling them back as she nodded. "You know, Margo said the same thing this morning, about Spencer. He told her that it was a good thing she's marrying a doctor since she keeps insisting on going on those risky hikes."

"See? The Stoker women know how to pick their other halves." Rhett dropped a kiss on her cheek.

"It's going to be okay. We can get takeout if you want. I'll call up to the Grill and put in an order. Or we can make sandwiches, I think there's some leftover shredded chicken from lunch. Maybe some taco shells in the pantry."

"Takeout sounds nice," Caroline admitted. She leaned her head back against Rhett's shoulder, allowing herself to luxuriate for just a moment in the feeling of him holding her. "I feel so behind on everything," she said quietly, still staring at the burned mess of casserole in the dish.

In the living room, she could still hear Toby happily babbling away, completely unaware of any stress she felt at the moment. That was a good thing, so it made her feel slightly better, along with the fact that Rhett's arms were still around her.

"I've been telling Mom for weeks that I would put the lawn ornaments and Christmas decorations up at the inn, and I haven't had time to do it," she admitted. "Normally it's all out the day after Thanksgiving. Mom and Dad can't go up to the attic any longer, and I would get Nora or Margo to help, but they're busy too, these days. And the guests are going to expect to start seeing Christmas decor soon."

"I can help," Rhett offered, and Caroline made a

soft noise of acknowledgement, turning to give him a peck on the cheek.

"I appreciate that. I really do. But I know exactly how Mom likes the decorating done, and we're both really particular about it, especially me. I'll get around to it."

For a moment, Rhett looked like he wanted to argue, but he nodded, leaning in to give her a kiss instead. She closed her eyes, and just as she expected to feel him kiss her—the shriek of the fire alarm interrupted them, making them both jump back.

Rhett started to laugh. "Hang on, I'll take care of it. Don't go anywhere," he told her, with mock firmness, and Caroline laughed.

"You don't have to worry about that. I have this to clean up."

But it didn't feel quite as daunting, now that she and Rhett had been laughing in the kitchen together. It hadn't shortened her to-do list at all, or changed the fact that they were going to eat dinner even later now, but it had made her feel less like everything was on the verge of toppling.

She should let herself enjoy things like that more, she told herself as she scraped the burnt casserole out into the garbage can. She had always struggled with letting herself relax and taking time for herself, but at least in the past, she'd had a more manageable to-do list and the time to do those things if she wanted to. Now, she usually felt like she didn't have the time to relax into those moments like coffee with her sisters or romantic moments with Rhett.

But she could tell that it helped. It was a good reminder.

"Do you remember the possessed smoke alarm at the inn that was the reason we met?" Rhett's voice cut through her thoughts as he walked back into the kitchen, and Caroline set the pan in the sink to soak as she turned around to face him.

"Of course I do," she said with a laugh. "It was so frustrating! I didn't have time to deal with it, and there didn't seem to be a reason for anything to be wrong. But it just kept going off, and you kept having to come and check on it. If I didn't know that it was that stupid electric furnace that was wired wrong, I'd think you'd rigged it so you could keep coming to see me," she added, poking him teasingly in the chest.

"I'd have done it if that's what it took." Rhett set his hands on her waist, leaning in to finally grab that kiss. "As persistently annoying as that smoke alarm was, it was worth it. And you didn't feel like you had time back then, but you handled it all just fine. I know you're going to keep doing that. I was impressed with you back then, and I still am now, all the time." He leaned down, kissing her again. "How about I go get us dinner from the Grill, and when I come back, Jay will be home and we can put Toby down for bed, and have a nice family dinner."

"I'd like that." Caroline smiled, feeling a little of the tension seep out of her shoulders.

"I'll call." Rhett went to sit at the kitchen table as Caroline finished washing what dishes she could from making dinner, and left the casserole pan to soak overnight. Just as Rhett was hanging up, probably to ask her what she wanted him to go and get for takeout, Jay came barreling through the front door.

"I'm home!' he yelled, his voice carrying through the house and making Toby let out a joyful screech. "And my homework's all done! Can we watch a movie tonight?"

Caroline looked anxiously at Rhett, who stood up and came over to give her another squeeze. "Sure thing, dude!" he called out to Jay. "Just run upstairs and get changed, and then we'll talk about it. We're having takeout for dinner, so you can come ride with me while I grab it."

"I have a lot to do tonight." Caroline bit her lip,

and Rhett reached down, taking both of her hands in his.

"I know. But it'll keep, and you'll be bummed out later if we miss out on one of these nights when we're all home, Jay doesn't have homework, and we can all spend time together. It's all right if the living room is a bit messy and all the decorations aren't up yet." He grinned at her. "Do you want me to get covered plates from Rockridge Grill? There's brisket, garlic mashed potatoes and roasted vegetables, or I can bring home the pot roast sandwiches and fries that are the special tonight?"

"Sandwiches and fries sound good. Get me some of that aioli that Jonathan makes? And I'll tidy up as much as I can until you get back."

Caroline let out a breath, telling herself it would be all right if some items got pushed to the next day. Rhett was right there, telling her that it would be all right, and after all, her family was what mattered most. Not her need to cross items off of a list or have everything around her just so.

"I can." Rhett hesitated, still holding her hands. "This is just a thought, sweetheart, but maybe you shouldn't be trying to do everything all by yourself anymore. Maybe it's time to look into hiring some help."

Caroline's eyes went wide. "I'm not hiring a *maid*!" she exclaimed, and Rhett chuckled.

"I know the idea of anyone but you cleaning your own house makes you twitchy. I don't mean for our house, I meant for the inn."

"Still..." Caroline was already shaking her head. "I don't know if I like the idea of bringing someone else in. The inn has always been family. We've always taken care of things ourselves. It's worked just fine that way for years."

"Yes, because you've always had someone in the family helping out," Rhett insisted gently. "For a long time, your parents ran things, and you helped. Then they started getting older, and you took over more, and it was more of you running things, and them helping. Nora moved back home, and she started to help out. Margo moved back home and moved into the inn, and I know she's helped you with a lot. But now your parents are slowing down, Nora has a baby and her own business to run, and Margo is getting married and branching out into her photography classes. It's starting to be just you, and that's a lot of pressure."

"It's just the holidays—"

"I know you want to think that." Rhett rubbed his thumbs over her knuckles soothingly. "And I know your parents are still in good health, and they do a lot. But they're going to want to enjoy some semblance of a retirement, although I don't think either of them are ever going to stop completely," he added with a chuckle. "Still, they're slowing down a bit. I don't want you to feel like you're missing out on time with Jay, and Toby's childhood, because you're so overwhelmed. I know you want to do it all, but you really don't have to."

Caroline pinched the bridge of her nose, considering his words. She knew, deep down, that he was giving her good advice. That she should listen. She *was* overwhelmed, and tired, and she did want to spend more time with her own family.

But she also knew that she liked things a certain way, and that it would be incredibly difficult to adapt to someone else doing those things. Not to mention the fact that whoever she hired would have to be a very patient person, to put up with how picky she would be for a long time, at least until she learned to let go of some of it.

"I'll think about it," she finally said, speaking slowly. "But *just* think about it. Okay?"

"That's all I ask," Rhett promised, giving her another soft kiss. "I'll go pick up dinner with Jay, give you a few more quiet minutes to knock some items off of your list. And then we'll have a nice family night in."

"Okay."

Caroline smiled, taking a deep breath as she watched him walk out, grabbing his truck keys and calling for Jay. But as she watched him go, she couldn't help wondering if she really could consider what he'd asked.

She had never imagined hiring a stranger to help out at the inn. But she had promised her husband that she would truly consider it.

So she would.

CHAPTER SIX

The wintry air was cold and crisp as Nora and Aiden walked out of Rockridge Grill Sunday evening after going out for dinner, just the two of them and Madison. Nora smiled to herself as she tucked Madison into the stroller with her coat and fuzzy hat, and blanket, thinking of the first date Aiden took her on, to Marie's. She hadn't even been sure that it was a date, back then, but as it turned out, it had been. Rockridge Grill was nowhere near as fancy as Marie's, and very far removed from the kind of fancy restaurants she used to go out to in Boston, but she didn't care. It was a perfect night out for the three of them.

It had been one of those nights where everything just seemed to fall into place too. The special had been Aiden's favorite—Jonathan's signature venison burgers with blue cheese crust and onion jam—and dessert had been Nora's favorite, toffee bread pudding with maple whipped topping. Madison had been perfect through it all, eating the mac and cheese that they'd gotten for her and tearing apart her fries, and she hadn't cried a bit. Now she was cooing in her stroller, playing with her reindeer in her mittened hands, and everything felt just right to Nora.

She honestly couldn't remember ever having been happier.

"Let's go for a nice evening walk," Aiden suggested, as he tugged on his leather gloves. "We can stop for hot chocolate at The Mellow Mug before Melanie closes up, and look at all the houses. Most of them should be decorated for Christmas by now."

"That sounds wonderful." Nora pushed the stroller as they started to walk a few storefronts down to The Mellow Mug. Melanie would be open for another thirty minutes or so, and she beamed as she saw Nora and Aiden walk in with Madison.

"Hey there!" she exclaimed, coming around the corner to lean down and wave to Madison. "I have a cookie for you. And the two of you want coffee this late?" she grinned as Nora shook her head.

"Hot chocolate? We were going to go on a little winter walk. Peppermint hot chocolate sounds amazing, actually."

"I'll take just normal hot cocoa," Aiden said with a grin, as Melanie got out a ginger cookie for Madison to gnaw on, while she started fixing their hot cocoa.

It was warm and pleasantly sugar scented in the coffee shop as they waited, and Nora looked around at the festive decorations, breathing in a deep lungful of the sweet air and feeling whatever remaining tension she might have had drain away. This was her favorite time of year for so many reasons. She'd loved it for a long time because of her job as an event planner. Every year, people threw parties and got married and had all kinds of big events surrounding the holiday.

She always loved seeing them come to life. But now it had taken on new meaning. Christmas was also the time of year when she'd come back home because she thought her life was falling apart, only to discover that it was starting over in a new way. It was the time of year that she'd fallen in love with Aiden. It was the time of year when she'd found herself adjusting to being a new parent, and when her family had finally been entirely reunited, and when she'd found out she was going to have a little niece to dote on. Every year, she was reminded of how her home had always been waiting for her, and how much love had been there when she'd finally come back.

Melanie handed her and Aiden their hot chocolates, and they headed back out into the winter evening. Main Street was fully decked out, with lights strung across the shops and arched over the streets, all of the lampposts decorated with wreaths and ribbons. They kept walking, sipping their hot cocoa as they walked out of the business part of town and into the residential area, where it was exploding with the lights and festivity of the holiday.

Aiden reached down, wrapping one gloved hand around hers as she pushed the stroller, side by side as their warm breaths puffed out in the air.

"I've always liked the holidays," he said as they walked. "But they really have become more special ever since you moved back home. Christmas became something much more to me, after that. Just like you became so much more to me that first Christmas you came home."

Nora smiled up at him, touching the compass

necklace that she always wore reflexively. "I was just thinking the same thing," she said softly. "This time of year really does bring us something new and special every year. I wonder what it will be this time."

"Another baby?" Aiden grinned at her, and Nora swatted him teasingly.

"Not yet. We've only just gotten this one sleeping. Remember last Christmas?"

"I'll never forget. That's how I know I really do want another one," he said with a grin. "Because I *do* remember, and I still want more babies with you. An even bigger family."

"I do too," Nora admitted. "Just maybe not yet. Although Margo told me that she thought I was really rocking the mom thing the other day, and I think she was right. *We* are really rocking this parenting thing. So maybe we can think about baby number two sooner rather than later." She grinned at him. "Seriously though, I'm so proud of how we figured out a rhythm. It was challenging, but we didn't let it get us down, and we pushed through it. And we came out so much stronger on the other side."

"I agree." Aiden leaned over, kissing her temple as they walked, and Nora smiled. She really did feel that their marriage was stronger than ever. Last year, as she and her sisters had worked to put together an anniversary surprise for their parents, she'd thought a lot about what made a truly successful marriage. About what made love last for years and years, the way her parents' had. And she'd come to the conclusion that she and Aiden had that. They had what it took to have the kind of marriage that would last, for their children growing up and their grandchildren too.

"Oh, look at that," Aiden commented as they rounded a corner toward another group of houses. "There's Bethany. I think she still has that puppy you mentioned."

Nora turned the stroller, walking closer. Bethany was standing in the front yard, a puppy on a leash as it relieved itself near one of the shrubs. As they walked into the lights coming from the lit-up snowmen in the yard, she could see that it was definitely the same puppy, fluffy and white with brown speckles, the floppy ears almost dragging in the snow.

"No luck finding the owner yet?" Nora asked as the three of them stopped, and Bethany looked up, shaking her head ruefully.

"No, unfortunately not."

"Going to keep her yourself?" Aiden asked with a chuckle, and Bethany shook her head quickly.

"I love her to bits," she said. "She's adorable and full of energy, but that's the thing. It's *too* much energy. And especially this time of year, with everyone wanting their pets groomed before the holidays even if they're not on their usual schedule, for Christmas card pictures, I just don't have enough time to give her the attention she needs. I'm working too much these days for a new baby in the house." She leaned down, petting the puppy, and the puppy let out a series of yipping barks as she tugged on the leash, trying to get to Madison.

Madison had fallen asleep as they'd walked, the remains of her ginger cookie in her lap, but she woke up immediately at the sound of the yipping. She clapped her mittened hands together, grinning widely and babbling to the puppy as she leaned forward in her stroller, reaching for it.

Bethany's face lit up as she looked at the baby and puppy trying to get to one another, and she looked up at Nora and Aiden. "I've just had a wonderful idea," she said with a grin. "What if you two took the puppy until I can find the owner, or someone who wants to adopt her long-term? It's clear that she and Madison have really taken to one another. I've never seen a dog get so excited over a baby. And Madison seems thrilled."

Nora took one look at Madison's wide grin and eager, grabbing hands, and knew she couldn't say no. "Okay," she said quickly, before she could over-think it. "We'll do it."

"Are you sure?" Aiden asked cautiously, looking down at the puppy bouncing in the snow. "We were just talking about how we'd gotten our stride with Madison. Won't a puppy be too much? You've just started getting your business running again, and you're planning Margo's wedding. A puppy this small will take a lot of time. Trips outside, training, and she's going to make messes and get into things. A lot of your decorations are going to have to be put up where she can't get to them."

"That's fine." Nora looked down at Madison and the puppy again. "Look how happy she is. It won't be too much trouble. And besides, we *do* have this down, remember? What's the addition of one little puppy?"

Aiden chuckled. "I did just say I wanted another baby. I suppose this is the easier of the two options. And you're right, Madison does seem to really love her. Anyway, it's only temporary, right?"

"Only temporary," Bethany agreed. "If I can't

find her owner soon, I'll put out some notices for adoption in the salon and around town. Someone will want to adopt her for good, I'm sure. It's just a matter of finding the right home. And until then, I think she'll be much better off with you."

"We'll have to stop by the general store and get stuff for her," Aiden said. "Food, puppy pads, that sort of thing. Maybe we should come back tomorrow, if that's all right? Pick her up then, so we can get ready. And puppy-proof the house tonight," he added. "It's already baby-proofed, but maybe another check wouldn't hurt."

"I can handle her for one more night," Bethany said with a laugh. "Tomorrow is fine."

"Tomorrow it is, then," Nora said. "Come on, Madison. We'll come back for the puppy tomorrow." She turned the stroller away as she said it, preparing for Madison's frustrated cries as they left the puppy behind, but Madison seemed to understand that they weren't leaving her forever. She let out another string of babbles as they walked away, and Aiden chuckled.

"Well then. Tomorrow we're getting a puppy."

Nora felt a thrill of excitement. She'd just been wondering what new thing this holiday season was going to bring for them. And it looked like she'd just found out.

CHAPTER SEVEN

Monday morning, Margo came downstairs to leave for work, surprised to see Melanie in the living room of the inn. She had a to-go mug of coffee in hand, animatedly chatting with Rhonda about something, and she looked up as Margo came down the stairs.

"Do you have a few minutes?" she asked, and Margo shrugged.

"Probably. Sabrina doesn't get upset if I'm a tiny bit late, especially on Mondays. Although I'm working on a new spread about winter hiking spots where you can get the best photos of wildlife in the area, so I definitely need to get there and start going through my photos sooner rather than later. What's up?"

"Well, besides wanting to come in and grab a

muffin..." Melanie held up the item in her other hand, a half-eaten cinnamon chip muffin that Margo knew was freshly baked. "I was at the general store this morning grabbing a few things for the coffee shop, and Leon happened to let it slip that your rings came in! They're all engraved and ready to go whenever you want to pick them up."

Margo's eyes widened. "Okay, I definitely have time to stop by before work, then. Sabrina will understand. Let's go get them! As soon as I grab some coffee," she added, hurrying into the kitchen with her thermos to load it up with peppermint mocha and whipped cream, and grab a muffin for herself. She'd already been running a little late this morning since she'd stayed up late reading by the fire the night before. She'd gotten a new magazine in, one with pictures of location and wildlife photography from all over, and she was already thinking of how she could use it for her next class. She also had a fun Christmas romance novel that had just been delivered, and between those two items, it had been well past midnight when she'd looked at the clock and realized that she needed to go to bed.

As a result, she definitely needed the extra caffeine this morning. And she was going to be probably an hour late for work by the time she was all done at Sugar Maple, but the rings would be a good enough explanation for Sabrina. Sabrina was as excited as everyone else about the wedding, especially since she'd been looking for someone to set Spencer up with about the time Margo had moved home two years ago. She credited herself with a lot of the romance that had started between the two of them, and whether or not that was strictly true, Margo let her believe it, since it clearly made her happy.

"Can I grab a ride with you?" Melanie asked. "I walked here from town since I needed a bit of exercise this morning, but now I'm cold and I would love to not have to walk back."

"Of course," Margo said with a laugh. "You don't even need to ask. Come on, let's go!"

Almost giddy with excitement, the two women piled into Margo's old Subaru and headed toward the Sugar Maple General Store. Margo pulled into the parking lot just as she finished her coffee, and the two of them jumped out of the car, almost giggling like little girls as they hurried in.

"I can't wait to see them," Melanie said. "I haven't gotten to see the rings at all yet! But Nora said that your mother told her that they're perfect. I'm so excited to see."

Leon grinned as soon as he saw the two girls walking in, clearly knowing just why they were there. "I've got your rings right here, Margo," he said, reaching under the counter to pull out the package. "Just like you asked. I put a bit of a rush on them too, no extra charge. So it didn't take long at all. I figured you'd be eager to have them back."

"I am," Margo assured him. "Thank you! Melanie, look."

She opened the packaging, sliding out the two blue velvet boxes and opening them. Side by side, the rings were just as perfect as she remembered. There was the white gold band with the diamonds set into it for her, and the plain band for Spencer. She slid each one out, seeing that the inscription was engraved on the inside in a pretty, flowing script, just as she'd requested.

My heart has found its home.

"Oh my goodness." Melanie pressed a hand to her chest as she read and reread it, finally handing the ring back to Margo. "It's perfect. And so romantic. I love it so much. Let me see it with your ring!"

Margo slipped the diamond band on next to her engagement ring, holding her hand out so that Melanie could squeal over it. Her heart tripped in her chest as Melanie took her hand and turned it back and forth, watching the light play over the stones. It really was beautiful, simple and perfect for her. She couldn't wait to wear it for the rest of her life.

"I've got another surprise for you too," Leon said with a grin. "All those decorations you and Nora ordered a few months ago? The tablecloths and lace doilies and such? Those all came in too. A whole carload of stuff, so we're going to need to take some time getting it all out there." He jerked a thumb toward the storage room behind him. "Came in yesterday evening, so I've got it all packed up back there."

"Nora is going to be so excited." Margo carefully slipped the bands back into their boxes, putting them in her bag as she looked expectantly toward the back room. "She's been waiting for them to come in. I'll text her as soon as we get them all loaded up."

There was a lot. Bethany came out of the salon a moment later, the fluffy puppy barking at her heels, and the four of them made three trips back and forth to Margo's car with bags stuffed full of tablecloths, doilies, ribbon, burlap, fake snow, votive candles, and items that Margo couldn't even remember Nora ordering.

One heavy box held the aisle runner she'd ordered, another was full of wide velvet ribbon to tie around all of the chairs. And all the while, as Leon sorted through to make sure that all of the packages were, in fact, the ones that were supposed to be going to Margo, the puppy barked and ran around, getting under everyone's feet as they danced around her and tried not to trip.

"Come here, Chessie!" Bethany called out, chasing her to grab her before she could run out into the snow as Leon opened up the door again for Melanie and Margo. "I keep calling her my little chestnut," she explained as she scooped the puppy up, cradling her as the last of the bags and boxes were carried out to Margo's Subaru. "The nickname seems to have stuck. I'll have to tell Nora about it when she comes to pick her up."

"Nora is taking her?" Margo looked at Bethany curiously, as the other woman nodded.

"She and Aiden were out for a walk last night and saw us outside. Madison has really taken to her, and Chessie seems to love her too, so I suggested they keep her while I'm trying to find either her owners or a new, permanent home. Nora loved the idea, and Aiden seemed to think it might work, so they're going to come pick her up today."

"I can't blame them. She's so cute." Margo reached out, scratching Chessie behind her ears. "And so fluffy. I can't imagine how anyone wouldn't want her."

"She is adorable," Bethany agreed. "But I'm glad Nora is picking her up this afternoon. I can't be doing all this running around. She's much better suited for someone with more energy, like Nora and a baby that will crawl and chase her around."

"That sounds entertaining." Margo gave Chessie one more scratch on her head, and then headed out with Melanie, to the car. She was definitely late for work by then, but she couldn't just leave the decorations there. She'd text Nora and have her come grab them after the puppy was all settled. Or she could drop them off at Nora's after work, she thought, and see Chessie again. She wanted to see the puppy and Madison chasing each other around. She couldn't think of many things that would be cuter than that.

On her way to *The Gazette*, she dropped Melanie off at The Mellow Mug, making a quick stop inside to grab a second coffee. She couldn't turn down the opportunity for her favorite maple cinnamon latte, and she had a feeling she was going to need the extra boost. She was already feeling sleepy after her late night.

Once at work, she grabbed several of the bags, carrying them into the office. She passed Sabrina as she walked in, who looked wide-eyed at Margo's haul, her cat's-eye glasses sliding down her nose.

"Ah. I see this is why you're late," she said with a laugh, and Margo gave her a rueful smile.

"Well, it started with the wedding rings. Leon got them back in, and I wanted to see the engravings. And then Leon said all of the decorations had come in, and I couldn't just *leave* them there, so I had to load all of those up."

"And now you're going to stash them where exactly?"

Sabrina arched a brow as she asked the question, but her eyes were twinkling, so Margo knew she wasn't upset. She was a gossip and a bit of a busybody—traits that she swore she was working on —but she was a romantic at heart, and Margo could see her eyeing the bags, probably wondering as to what had been ordered for the wedding.

"In my office. Where no one else will see them," Margo promised. "I just don't want it all sitting out in the cold. There's votive glass and stuff like that, which is breakable and might not react well to low temperatures. I'm going to see if Nora can either come pick it all up, or I'll take it to her place after work. She's taking in that puppy that Bethany found, so she might be busy for a bit this afternoon."

"Oh, I heard about that. I saw that little baby when I stopped in the other day." Sabrina sighed. "If my other half would let me, I would have taken that puppy home. But no more pets in our household. Not right now anyway."

"Well, Madison and Chessie apparently adore each other," Margo said with a laugh. "So Nora is going to watch her for now. And Bethany seems pretty relieved. Seems like puppy duty is wearing her out."

"I don't blame her." Sabrina glanced at the bags again. "When you're done stashing all of that, come give me an update on your article."

"Will do." Margo flashed her a grin, and started carrying the bags into her office.

Twenty minutes later, it was all stashed in one corner near her filing cabinet. She looked at the pile of bags and boxes, feeling a thrill as her heart tripped in her chest. With every day that passed, and every little thing that made it feel more real, she could feel herself getting more and more excited for the wedding.

She couldn't wait to marry Spencer.

CHAPTER EIGHT

That afternoon, Nora arrived with Madison all bundled up, ready to pick up Chessie.

She came in through the general store since she wanted to get some things from Leon. She knew that Bethany would probably give her everything that she needed for Chessie, at least to start, but she wanted to be extra prepared. So she grabbed a new dog bed—a cute, bone-shaped one in green and red that looked very festive—and some puppy treats and a few squeaky toys.

There was a Christmas stocking in a mink-like fabric that had a crinkly texture inside, and a squeaky bone, as well as a stuffed lamb. She had Leon bag them all up, just as she heard the connecting door open and saw Bethany walk in with Chessie squirming in her arms.

Aiden had been a little worried about agreeing to take the puppy that morning. He'd questioned if maybe they'd made a snap decision the night before, influenced by how perfect and romantic the night had been, as well as his musings about expanding their family and how adorable Madison had been with Chessie.

He pointed out that Madison was too little to actually realize that they'd agreed to take the puppy, so she wouldn't be disappointed if they backed out. He'd expressed his concerns again that it might be too much since Nora would be doing the bulk of the work, taking care of both baby and puppy while he was working his long days at the carpentry business.

Nora was convinced that it would be a breeze though. After conquering Madison's sleep schedule last Christmas, she felt sure that a puppy couldn't be even half as difficult as that had been. And the thought of how happy it made Madison made her sure that it was the right plan.

Still, she couldn't help but notice how frazzled Bethany looked as she carried Chessie out to her. Madison let out an excited squeal the instant she saw the puppy, and Nora felt that that was just confirmation that she'd made the right decision. Madison was already clapping her hands and reaching out for Chessie before Bethany had even passed her over to Nora.

"She's been barking and running around all morning," Bethany said, pushing a loose lock of hair behind her ear. "Getting all the other dogs that come in worked up. She has pretty much boundless energy, although that's usual for a puppy her age. You'll have your hands full, wearing her out."

"She'll have the whole house to run around in." Nora took Chessie, smiling as the furry puppy curled up in her arms, squirming happily and trying to lick her face. "I'm sure she won't be an inconvenience at all."

"Well, if anything goes wrong, just give me a call," Bethany said. "I don't want you to feel that you're locked into this, or anything. If it does prove to be too much, I'll take her back until I can find her a home."

"I'm sure it will be fine," Nora reassured her, gathering up Chessie along with the bag of supplies, and giving Bethany a smile before heading back out into the bright winter afternoon.

Excited and a little anxious to get back, she took her baby and their—temporary—new puppy home.

* * *

Mid-morning on Tuesday, Caroline drove to The Mellow Mug, tapping her fingers nervously on the steering wheel to the sound of the Christmas music playing in the car the whole way. Fidgety as she was, she ordered her favorite cinnamon Americano and found a table near the window. She stared at her cup as she picked apart a maple cinnamon roll, anxious and wishing that her coffee would hurry up and cool down so that she would have something to distract her.

She'd made the mistake, after Rhett had urged her to think about hiring help for The Mistletoe Inn, of talking to Nora and Margo about it. She'd felt sure that as soon as she sat down with the two of them over lunch and told them about Rhett's ridiculous idea, they would reassure her that it wasn't at all necessary, that she was doing just fine, and that she was completely justified in not wanting help outside of the family to come in and start fussing around the inn.

Instead, they'd agreed with Rhett. She'd felt a little betrayed at first over the whole thing, feeling that as her sisters, they should have agreed with her from the jump. But Nora and Margo had both pointed out the same things that Rhett had. Their parents were slowing down, and after a lifetime of working hard and putting their all into the inn, they deserved to get to enjoy that slower pace.

Nora had pointed out that she could no longer come by as much as she once had, with Madison, the wedding planning, and reviving her own business. She'd used to come by the inn almost every morning for coffee and breakfast, now she only made it over a couple of times a week, outside of scheduled family dinners. Margo pointed out that she too, would be moving out of the inn soon after the wedding, and with planning it and her photography classes and job, she hadn't had much time to lend a hand.

And they'd finished it up with a reminder that Caroline had *two* children to raise now, a stepson who was rapidly becoming a teenager, and a brand new baby. The two most difficult phases of childhood, Nora had told her with a laugh, and also the ones filled with all the biggest milestones. Margo had reminded Caroline that while she had always thrown herself fully into the work of the inn, she couldn't give her whole life to it. And she shouldn't. She had her own life as a wife and a mother now, and she should get to enjoy that too.

As much as she'd wanted to totally toss all of that

out of the window, Caroline had to admit that her sisters had valid points. She *had* always had some form of help, in her parents or sisters. And now that help from those sources was tapering off, for a variety of reasons, she couldn't expect herself to keep up the pace of running everything almost single-handedly forever.

She looked at her phone as her coffee finally cooled down enough to drink, re-reading the string of text messages that she had between her and the woman that she had finally settled on an interview with—a woman in her late thirties named Shelby Nussle. She'd put out a few feelers in town, trying to find out if anyone she knew also knew of someone looking for a part-time job.

Her best friend, Audrey, had said that her husband's cousin Shelby had just moved into town, and was looking for work. She'd given Caroline a glowing recommendation, assuring her that Shelby would be perfect for the job, and it had been the only recommendation Caroline had felt comfortable following up on.

After all, Audrey knew Caroline better than anyone, other than her family and Rhett. If Audrey thought that this Shelby would be able to tolerate Caroline's pickiness, and that they'd work well together, then Caroline thought that there was a good chance that was actually the case.

It was clear that Shelby was someone who was energetic, disciplined, and used to hard work. She had been a track athlete in high school, college, and afterward, according to the resume that she'd sent Caroline, and she'd worked as a coach for high school track in Burlington until very recently. On paper, and via her references, she seemed like exactly the sort of person that Caroline would want to hire.

Still, she couldn't feel sure that the meeting would come to anything. She wasn't sure that she wanted it to. But she had to admit that she couldn't keep going the way she was. And just the thought of how many of Toby's firsts that she might not be enjoying to their fullest because she was so distracted made her throat tighten, every time it popped into her head.

She needed more time to soak up this stage of his life. And Jay's teenage years, which were going to be full of as many milestones as Toby's first years, as Nora and Margo had reminded her. She didn't want them to grow up remembering that she had always been working, more than anything else.

Looking up, she saw a woman that she didn't recognize standing at the end of the counter, waiting on her coffee. The woman looked to be in her late thirties, with short brown hair pulled back in a neat ponytail, wearing a pair of workout leggings and a long, soft-looking dark red sweater, with duck boots. She looked in Caroline's direction a moment later, green eyes bright, and a big smile crossed her face as she waved eagerly to Caroline with one hand and grabbed her coffee with the other.

"It's so nice to meet you!" she exclaimed as she sat down. "Shelby Nussle. I haven't been here long, but I already love this coffee shop. They have the *best* peppermint mocha. It's even better than my little spot back in Burlington."

"Caroline Donovan." Caroline held out a hand, and Shelby shook it enthusiastically. "Audrey told me you might be interested in the job."

"Oh, yes." Shelby nodded, taking a sip of her coffee. "Audrey is the best, isn't she? I've really been enjoying getting to know her better. She and Ted were lovely enough to let me crash at their place until I could find something of my own to rent. Not a lot of apartments here in Evergreen Hollow. But I think I'll be looking for something to buy soon enough. Anyway, that's not what I'm here to talk about. The job." She refocused, smiling brightly, and

Caroline couldn't help but think that at the very least, Shelby had the energy for it.

"Tell me a little about yourself. You were a track runner and a coach? What brought you back here?"

"Well..." Shelby took another sip of her coffee, settling in. "I did track in high school, and went to college on a scholarship for it. I kept competing after college, until a knee injury made me quit. After that, coaching seemed like the next logical choice. I love kids, and I loved the sport, so I thought that would be perfect for me. And it was, but honestly, I started to feel burned out by all of it. I went through some big life changes—a breakup, friends moving away, you know the sort of thing—and I thought maybe I needed a more drastic change for myself. I felt like I needed new scenery, something quieter. Somewhere that I could think about what *my* personal dreams are now that I'm not running track any longer, you know?"

"I can understand that." Caroline glanced down at her resume. "You do have some experience in hospitality though."

"Yes!" Shelby nodded eagerly. "I worked for a bed and breakfast in Burlington all through college, to supplement what my scholarship gave me. I loved it, honestly. I liked interacting with the guests, hearing their stories about where they'd traveled from and what brought them there, all of that. I was sad to leave after college, honestly. But the place was downsizing, and I had to travel for track, so it didn't work out for me to stay."

"I see." Caroline sat back, taking another long sip of her Americano. "This is part-time, for now at least, and probably for the foreseeable future. Evergreen Hollow definitely isn't as expensive of a place to live as Burlington, but the salary probably won't cover all your expenses. And I'll need the schedule for the inn to take priority. Is that possible?"

Shelby nodded. "I've been doing some article writing, sort of freelance work on the side. I can easily schedule that around when you need me at the inn."

Caroline let out a slow breath as she scanned the resume once more, thinking. On paper, Shelby was as perfect as Audrey had made her out to be. She was enthusiastic, had some experience, was friendly, and flexible. Caroline knew she should hire her, but she still felt hesitant. The inn was like her child, and she couldn't help but feel that she was turning part of it over to a stranger after she'd spent so much of her life carefully tending it at all times.

"I think I'd be a great addition," Shelby added.

"I'd really like to come work for you, Mrs. Donovan. I've seen the inn from the outside, and it's so cute. I'd love to work there."

Slowly, Caroline nodded. "Alright," she said finally. "We'll do a two-week trial period. I'll let you know, this is one of the busiest times of the year, so be prepared. It will be quite hectic. And I'm very particular about how things are done."

"So were my employers at the place in Burlington," Shelby said with a smile. "No worries there. It's your place, so of course you are. I'm just going to be happy to learn how you like it all done."

"I'll see you bright and early Thursday, then," Caroline said. "If that works?"

"Absolutely." Shelby's smile brightened. "See you then!"

As Caroline watched her go, she hoped that she'd made the right decision. She knew that Rhett and her sisters had been right to encourage her to bring someone else on.

But that didn't mean that it would be easy to make that leap.

CHAPTER NINE

Nora dusted her hands off on her jeans as she pulled a baking sheet of molasses cookies out of the oven, breathing in the fragrant, Christmassy scent as she carefully listened for sounds of either Madison or Chessie.

Madison was down for the night, and Aiden had just gotten home from work—-she could hear the sound of the shower running upstairs as he got cleaned up. He'd eaten takeout from Rockridge Grill on the worksite, working late on some repairs with Blake for a neighbor's house, and she'd had dinner by herself that evening, eating lasagna while Madison happily painted the tray of her high chair with peas.

Now that dinner was over and Madison was

sleeping, she was eager to get some alone time with Aiden, just the two of them.

She'd gotten Chessie situated in the living room, in her own little corner with the dog bed and her toys, and a small playpen fence around it to keep her from having unfettered access to all parts of the house when Nora couldn't watch her. She'd had to pick up several of the decorations in order to make it completely safe for the puppy, but she hadn't minded a bit. Watching Madison scoot over the floor after Chessie earlier that afternoon, as the puppy had run in circles around her, had been adorably entertaining. And Madison was so happy that Nora couldn't regret the choice for a second.

Now Chessie was sleeping too, completely worn out and curled up in her dog bed. Which left Nora to put some of the freshly baked cookies on a small Christmas China plate, and set it on a tray with two cups of decaf pumpkin chai for herself and Aiden, ready to go out onto the porch and enjoy them.

It was the perfect winter night to do exactly that. Aiden came downstairs in sweats and a zip-up hoodie, and he carried the tray out as Nora gathered up blankets for them to curl up together out on the porch swing. It was cold, but wrapped up in the blankets as Aiden set the tray down on the small table that he'd made for them last year, Nora hardly felt the cold at all.

The sky was clear of clouds, bright and sparkling with stars, the snowy front yard lit up with the lights strung across the front of their old Victorian and wrapped around the porch. She could see the lights from other houses as well, spilling out over the snow, and she let out a happy sigh as she reached for her cup of chai and one of the cookies.

"Is this your mom's recipe?" Aiden asked as he took a bite. "I feel like I've had these before."

"Yes." Nora nodded, laughing as she took a bite out of her cookie as well. "I think I've finally perfected it."

"I would agree." He sipped on his chai, letting out a relaxed sigh. "What a perfect night. This kind of evening is exactly why I love living here. It's so peaceful."

"It is." Nora tucked her feet up under her, leaning against him as she sipped her drink. "I thought the quiet would drive me crazy after living in Boston for so long, when I first moved back. But I love it. It makes me feel like I can slow down and think. And they're all good thoughts. Our life here is so good."

"And just getting better. Everything seems to be

going well with managing both Madison and Chessie too." Aiden smirked at her. "You're juggling it all remarkably well. Not a peep from either of them tonight. You've become an expert at wearing out babies *and* puppies."

"It's a breeze," Nora said smugly, a teasing look on her face as she brushed her hair back playfully. "You just have to be organized, that's all."

"Oh, is that it?" Aiden grinned. "Perfect for you, then. You're the most organized person I've ever met. Even when you were running on almost no sleep with Madison, I still don't think I ever met anyone who could keep things in order as well as you—"

He broke off, as they both heard a whine from inside the house, long and high-pitched, followed by a flurry of frenzied barking.

"Oh, no." Nora set her mug down. "What's going on with her? She's slept great ever since we brought her home. I don't know what's got her all upset now."

Aiden shrugged, as the barking went on, growing more and more frantic by the second. "She was probably exhausted when you first brought her back here," he reasoned. "And now she's gotten used to her surroundings, so she wants to play. She'll settle down in a minute."

Nora bit her lip, giving it another second or two,

but as the frenzied barking continued, she pushed off the blankets and got up. "I've got to go quiet her down before she wakes Madison up," she said. "I'll be right back."

"I can do it," Aiden offered, but Nora shook her head.

"No, it's okay. I've spent more time with her, so she might calm down better for me. The two of you still need to get acquainted, really. And I don't want to end our romantic evening just yet. I'll be right back, promise."

She hurried into the house, where the barking was even more high-pitched. She went straight to the small enclosure, scooping Chessie up and grabbing her harness and leash. "Do you just need to go out?" she asked, nuzzling the top of the puppy's head as she took her to the back door. "Maybe that's it."

As soon as she was holding the puppy, she noticed, Chessie stopped barking. Hopefully, she wasn't going to start again as soon as Nora set her down.

She put the harness on, walked out into the backyard, and let Chessie run around in a few circles before she finally did her business next to a snowdrift. Nora scooped her back up, not wanting her paws to get too cold, and carried her back into the house and to her dog bed.

"There," she said, setting her down and unclipping the harness. "You're all good now, okay? Let's go back to sleep. I want some time to wind down before *I* have to go to sleep too."

She petted Chessie's head as she spoke soothingly, and the puppy laid down, rolling onto her side as Nora scratched her chest and behind her leg. When she could see the puppy's eyes drooping, she set the harness aside and softly walked back out to the porch, where Aiden was taking a bite out of another cookie.

"All good?" he asked, and Nora nodded.

"She just needed to go out. I'm pretty sure that's all it was," she said confidently. "And that's good, right? She told me, instead of having an accident. That's what we want her to do."

"Although maybe not so loudly," Aiden said with a good-natured chuckle. "But you're right. That's definitely what we want."

Nora settled back into the cocoon of blankets, picking up a second cookie for herself and taking another sip of her now-cooled chai tea. She was just starting to relax again when she heard the telltale whine of Chessie warming up, and then the sudden flurry of barking that immediately followed.

"Is this reminding you of anything?" Aiden asked dryly, as Nora sighed and pushed back the blankets again.

"You're the one who said you wanted another baby already," she teased him. "This is just a trial run, to make sure we remember, and can handle it."

"I think the barking is worse," Aiden said, but Nora could tell he wasn't overly annoyed by it. "I guess we should go ahead and turn in. Until you figure out what she wants, it's not going to stop."

"No, wait," Nora insisted. "I'll go check on her, and come back."

She could tell that Aiden didn't think the puppy would settle, but he indulged her. He curled back up in the blankets, tucking them around him and nestling Nora's section of blankets close to keep them warm as she went back into the house.

"Okay, you," she said to Chessie, walking back over to where the puppy was pressed up against the edge of the playpen, barking wildly. "It's bedtime, little girl. And you can't just have the run of the house. I'll find accidents and chewed furniture in the morning, I know I will. You can run around with Madison tomorrow."

Chessie started barking again, and Nora sighed, scooping the puppy up. The second she was in Nora's arms, she quieted down, and Nora winced.

There definitely was some separation anxiety going on, she thought. But she couldn't constantly hold Chessie. For one thing, she needed to hold *Madison* sometimes. For another, she had chores to do. For a third, as happy as she was to have the puppy, she couldn't have Chessie constantly glued to her.

"Let's try this." She scooped up the little lamb, remembering that she'd read on the tag that it could be tossed in a microwave for a few seconds to heat up the stuffed animal, making it warm and soothing. "Maybe you just need a cuddle buddy."

She held Chessie while the stuffed animal warmed up, letting the puppy lick the edges of her chin as she squirmed happily in Nora's arms. When the microwave beeped, Nora took the lamb out, taking both it and Chessie back to the small bed next to the fireplace and getting them situated again.

After a few minutes of petting, Chessie seemed content to curl up with the warmed-up stuffed lamb, and Nora let out a sigh. Carefully, she went back out to the porch, where she found Aiden reading as he waited for her.

"Not too chilly are you?" she asked as she nestled back into her blankets.

"Now that you're back, I'm great." He leaned over to give her a soft kiss. "How's the baby?"

Nora rolled her eyes playfully. "I warmed up her stuffed animal. I think maybe she's just got some attachment issues. That should help."

The night was back to being quiet as she curled up with Aiden on the swing, nibbling at her cookie and enjoying the crisp, cold scent of the winter air and the scenery all around them. She could smell the far-off scent of someone's bonfire, the spiciness of the chai still in her cup, and the warmth of the molasses cookies. She closed her eyes without meaning to, feeling herself drift off a little as the swing rocked back and forth.

She came awake with a start as Aiden rubbed her back gently. "You fell asleep," he said with a chuckle. "We should probably be getting to bed."

"Alright," Nora agreed, yawning. "You're probably right."

As quietly as they could, they both gathered up the dishes and blankets, and carried them to the linen closet and kitchen. Nora waited the whole time for Chessie to wake up and start barking again, but to her relief, the puppy stayed asleep. It seemed that the heated stuffed animal might have done the trick.

Until, a few hours later, Nora was awoken from a deep sleep by the insistent sound of Chessie barking downstairs. She sat up, pushing her hair out of her face as Aiden groaned, and threw the blankets back. Quickly, she shoved her feet into her slippers and started to pad downstairs to get the puppy to calm down, but before she could get more than a few steps past the landing, Madison started to wail from the nursery as well.

Nora wrinkled her nose, her shoulders sinking. Behind her, she could hear Aiden getting out of bed, undoubtedly going to get the baby while she went to calm down Chessie.

The barking turned frantic, and Nora quickened her pace, Madison's cries echoing behind her as she hurried into the living room.

It was going to be a long night.

CHAPTER TEN

Margo pushed aside the stack of papers and her open laptop, making a spot for the plate of sandwiches that she'd just fixed for lunch. Nora was coming over to go through the fine details of the wedding planning with her—all that they had left to do, really—and she was buzzing with excitement. So much so that she'd told Nora to let her make lunch for them, as a way to burn off some of that excess energy, instead of Nora picking up takeout from Rockridge Grill like they'd originally planned. Nora had sounded oddly relieved, which had surprised Margo, but Nora had gotten off of the phone so quickly, promising not to be late, that she hadn't had time to ask about it.

Nora *was* running about ten minutes late. But Margo wasn't worried about it. Nora would turn up eventually, and in the meantime, she'd had extra time to perfect lunch.

She'd been crazy about a special that Rockridge Grill had run right after Thanksgiving last year: a turkey sandwich with cranberry sauce, cream cheese, and a bit of leftover gravy on it with caramelized onions. Since then, she'd been trying to figure out how to replicate it, and she thought she'd finally gotten it down. Between that and the leftover butternut squash bisque that Rhonda had made to go with dinner the night before, Margo thought she'd managed to assemble a pretty good winter lunch.

While she waited, she sat back down and looked over her spreadsheet again, one that Nora had originally put together and then shared with her. It outlined what needed to be at every guest's chair for the wedding ceremony, and then at their dinner seat for the reception. Everything from the disposable camera for the pictures at both places, to the handcrafted box with the small favors, to how the dinner settings should be arranged. Margo was honestly impressed, every time she looked at it. She'd known her sister would be good at anything she did for a career, of course, but she'd never realized just how amazing Nora was at her job until they'd started planning this wedding.

The fine attention to detail was something she would never have pulled off on her own. She could make sure an article was copy-edited to perfection, find every little detail in a photo that needed to be highlighted or edited so the finished product was exactly right for a magazine spread, but trying to keep track of how many favors needed to go in each box, seating charts, and which floral arrangements were at which tables would have driven her nuts from the start. But Nora definitely thrived on it.

A moment later, just as she was beginning to worry that lunch would get too cold, she heard the tell-tale sound of boots knocking against the mat outside. The door opened a minute later, and Nora blew in, clearly more than a little frazzled. She didn't have her gloves on, and her normally smoothly styled dark hair was spilling out of a hastily assembled messy bun on top of her head. Her face was flushed, and she seemed out of breath as she kicked off her boots.

She was also toting Madison in one arm—who was equally red-faced and looked on the verge of bursting into screams—and a familiar-looking white and brown puppy in the other, who was squirming even more than Madison.

Margo jumped up immediately to help. "What's

going on?" she asked concernedly, although it seemed obvious that the addition of Chessie was proving to be more than a handful. She was sure that Rhonda wouldn't mind having the puppy around, although she could already hear Caroline's concerns about whether or not Chessie might chew or pee on something she wasn't supposed to. It was probably better, honestly, if Caroline didn't see the puppy. But she was pretty sure that Caroline was down at the cottage for lunch, feeding Toby and making lunch for Jay, who would be in from sledding with his friends for lunch. Possibly *with* his friends, who would all be hungry.

Nora let out a breath, and Margo could see the dark circles under her sister's eyes. She hadn't looked this tired since the holidays last year, when she hadn't been able to get Madison to sleep on a regular schedule, and hadn't had a normal sleep schedule of her own either.

"I'm sorry to drag all this along," Nora said. "I know we were supposed to have some time with just the two of us this afternoon. But Aiden had to go to an emergency meeting about some repairs, and—"

"It's absolutely fine," Margo assured her sister quickly. "Here, give me Madison, and I'll get her settled over here in the armchair. I have a bunch of stuffed animals she can play with, I'll just go grab them really quick. And Mom has some homemade mac-and-cheese in the refrigerator for quick snacks, there's a couple staying here who have two kids, and she made it for them. But they've barely touched it, so they won't miss a bowl. I'll heat some up for Madison if she gets hungry."

"Thank you so much." Nora gave Margo a look of relief, shrugging off the rest of her outerwear with Chessie still squirming in her arms.

"You can let her run around too," Margo offered. "Mom won't care, and Caroline is down at her house. I'll be right back."

Nora dropped into one of the armchairs, still clearly unsure about letting Chessie have the run of the inn. Margo went upstairs to grab a few stuffed animals that she'd collected over the years from various places, as well as two that she'd planned on giving Madison for Christmas. Madison was too small still, she figured, to realize that they'd show up again under the tree.

A few minutes later, Madison was settled in the armchair, surrounded by stuffed animals and particularly enamored of one that made small, high-pitched growls every time she pressed the paw. Margo grinned as she sank back down onto the couch. "That's her Christmas present," she whispered in a theatrical tone. "I'm glad to see I picked right."

Nora smiled tiredly, finally setting Chessie down on the floor. "You made lunch?" she asked with a hint of surprise, finally seeing the spread on the table, and Margo laughed.

"You don't have to sound so shocked!"

"You're really getting ready for this whole being-a-wife thing." Nora smirked. "Is it edible?"

"I certainly hope so." Margo reached out, dividing the sandwiches onto two smaller plates and handing one to Nora. "I've been trying to get this recipe right for a year."

"What did you make to drink?" Nora peered at the fizzy beverage in one of the green-hued Christmas drink glasses that Rhonda always brought out this time of year, and Margo grinned.

"Another step on the road to domesticity. I added ginger soda to some iced apple spice tea. I think it's really good."

Nora took a cautious bite of her sandwich, then a sip of her drink, and let out a happy hum of enjoyment. "That's really good, Margo!" she said, taking another bite, and Margo beamed.

"The soup is leftovers from Mom, so of course

it's good too. But I'm so glad you like the lunch!" She reached for her own sandwich, and just as she did, Chessie leapt up on the couch, climbing into Margo's lap and making a quick circle before curling up and promptly falling asleep. All before Margo even had time to take a bite out of her turkey sandwich.

Nora sighed as she set hers down, reaching for the bowl of soup. "I wish she would do that at night."

Margo frowned, taking in her sister's frazzled appearance again. "How are things going?" she asked cautiously, and Nora glanced between Chessie and Madison before dipping her spoon into her soup bowl.

"It's been quite the morning," Nora admitted. "And quite the night last night. We brought Chessie home yesterday, and she seemed fine until nighttime. Then Aiden and I were trying to have a few peaceful moments out on the porch after Madison went down, and Chessie started barking nonstop. I tried taking her out again, tried warming up a little stuffie for her—and it all worked for a little while. Then we went to bed, and she started up again. Woke Madison up."

"Mm." Margo frowned. "Sounds familiar."

Nora groaned. "That's what Aiden said. It was all night, up and down. I figured at least today,

Madison would probably sleep all day. But I guess having her sleep schedule messed up made her cranky too, because, for the first time in a really long time, she fought her nap. Wouldn't go to sleep at all, even though I *know* she's as exhausted as I am."

"Did you try that silly song?" Margo grinned, recalling the lightbulb moment Aiden had had last year that had finally cracked the code of getting Madison to fall asleep. "What was it? *I Want A Hippopotamus For Christmas?*"

"Not even that," Nora sighed. "Nothing soothed her at all. Finally, I just gave up and decided to let her stay up. Maybe she'll be so tired by tonight that she'll sleep even if Chessie goes crazy and barks again."

"Have you thought about telling Bethany?" Margo asked cautiously. "Maybe it's just not a good time for a puppy. I bet someone else—"

Nora shook her head. "Madison adores Chessie. I'm actually a little concerned with how upset she'll be when Bethany does find a forever home for her. I don't want to just give up after one night. Plus, we figured this out with a baby. How hard can a puppy possibly be?"

"Now it's a baby *and* a puppy," Margo pointed

out, and Nora laughed, taking another bite of her sandwich.

"Still, we'll figure out how to calm them both down. Maybe Aiden will figure out the magic trick for a dog too." Nora set her plate down as she finished the last of her food. "Honestly, this is amazing, Margo. You should make it for Spencer sometime."

"I will, now that I have it down. It's a lunch he brought me from the Grill last season, so he'll find it very romantic, I'm sure." Margo grinned, collecting the plates. "I'll clean up and then we can get down to planning."

When she came back out, Nora was sorting through the spreadsheet. In the armchair, surrounded by the plushies, Madison was asleep. And Chessie had curled up by the edge of the couch, chewing happily on a bone that Nora had brought along. It was a picture-perfect, quiet moment, and Margo smiled, taking it in. She was so glad that she had her sister here to help her with this. And she didn't mind the extra company a bit either.

"Thank you for coming even though it's been crazy all day for you," Margo said, sitting back down and putting fresh glasses of the apple soda out for them. "I would have understood if you'd begged off."

"Not a chance," Nora said firmly. "I'm thrilled to help. This is the most fun wedding gift I could possibly have come up with for you." She scrolled through the spreadsheet again, looking at it with an eagle eye. "And I think everything's here. All in order, just the way I wanted. We'll be able to set up like a breeze with this." She set the laptop back down, glancing over at Margo with a smile, clearly more relaxed now. "Melanie told me that the rings came in and she saw the engravings! She said they turned out great."

"Oh my gosh, yes!" Margo got up quickly, careful of where Chessie was still lying near her feet and happily chewing away. "I can show them to you. I'll go grab them, hang on."

She hurried upstairs to her bedroom, where she'd stashed them in the nightstand. But when she opened the drawer, the blue velvet boxes that she'd expected to see weren't there.

Her heart stuttered in her chest, and she frowned, hurrying over to her dresser. Maybe she'd stashed them there instead, and just *thought* that she'd put them in the nightstand. But as she dug through all of the drawers, sifting through her clothes, she couldn't find the rings anywhere.

Now actually worried, she went into the

bathroom, looking through the medicine cabinet and her toiletry bag, feeling like a squirrel with an acorn. She'd wanted to put them somewhere that Spencer wouldn't accidentally see them if he came over, but now it seemed like she'd hidden them from herself too.

She was starting to feel more than a little panicked when she'd searched all over her bedroom and bathroom, and couldn't find anything.

As soon as she came back downstairs, Nora saw her panicked face. "What's wrong?" she asked confusedly, and Margo threw up her hands.

"I can't find the rings. I *know* I put them in my nightstand drawer, I *remember* doing it, but they're not there. And I can't find them anywhere else in my room. I swear I remember bringing them home."

"Maybe you just need a second pair of eyes. Nora walked over to Madison, who was just starting to wake up, and gently scooped her up. "Grab Chessie, and let's both go up to your room. I'll help you look."

That made Margo feel a little better. She'd just missed them, and surely with Nora looking too, they'd find the rings in no time.

But no matter how much they both looked, they couldn't find them anywhere. Nora set Madison down on the floor next to Chessie, letting the two chase each other around in hopes that she could look better without distractions, but it was no use. And in the middle of it all, Margo felt her phone buzz in her pocket.

She pulled it out and saw it was Spencer calling. Her stomach dropped as she answered, holding up a finger to her lips to tell Nora not to say anything about the rings.

"Hey there," she said, trying not to sound as worried as she felt. "What's going on?"

"I was just on my lunch." There was the rustling of a bag in the background. "I was thinking, what if we go out tonight? I know you're crazy busy with the wedding planning, but I thought we could go to Marie's and then see the tree in the center of town. Melanie is keeping the coffee shop open late tonight for a live music event, we could go to that too."

"Marie's?" Margo teased, looking nervously at Nora as her sister pawed through another drawer, coming up empty-handed. "Any particular reason?"

"I just thought a nice night out would be a treat. I bought a new sweater." Spencer laughed. "But really, we haven't been out anywhere fancy in a while. I was craving something a little more upscale tonight, I think."

"I love that idea," Margo said firmly. "It's a date."

She hung up a moment later, looking at Nora as her sister turned to face her, holding up her hands helplessly. "I can't find them either," Nora said, and Margo let out a frustrated sigh.

"They've got to be somewhere." She shoved her phone back into her pocket, her hands on her hips. "I *have* to find those rings."

CHAPTER ELEVEN

Shelby's first day helping out at the inn had gone smoothly, but Caroline couldn't help hovering.

She *knew* she was hovering too. And she knew she should just give Shelby a tour and give her space to prove that she could do all of the tasks without issue, but Caroline felt like a mother hen. She'd never let anyone who wasn't a part of the family help out before, and it made her unaccountably nervous. Even the maintenance was usually done by her and Donovan, unless it was something truly out of their skill set like repairing the roof. And even then, Aiden, her brother-in-law, had been the one who had headed up that project.

It just felt extremely difficult to let anyone she

didn't know and who wasn't a part of the Stoker family—or part of it by extension—help with the running of The Mistletoe Inn. She couldn't wrap her head around just being okay with it.

Shelby turned up bright and early at eight a.m., when Caroline had requested, just in time for Caroline to come in from feeding the animals. She gave Shelby a tour of the kitchen first, showing her which refrigerator was for family and which was for the guests, and gave her a rundown of the usual schedule.

"Breakfast starts being served at nine in the morning," Caroline told her, showing Shelby an example of the pretty menus that were on the inn's website and also given to each guest as they checked in, as well as being available to view in the guests' dining room. Right now, for the Christmas season, they were printed on rustic brown paper with holly decorating the edges. "The menu changes weekly, and it's based on the season and what's available locally. That's important if guests have questions. The fact that all guest meals are sourced locally is one of the selling points of staying here, so it's important to remember that."

Shelby glanced down the menu, which at the

moment offered options of steel-cut oats with cranberries and dried orange slices, pumpkin cream cheese or cinnamon chip muffins, maple brioche French toast with local sausage links, eggs Benedict with local ham, homemade Hollandaise and eggs from the inn's chickens, and a breakfast wrap made with local chorizo, local vegetables, goat cheese, and again, eggs from the inn.

"I think I'd stay here just for the breakfast," Shelby declared when she was done looking it over. "I've kept my figure from my running days, but this might just put an end to that."

Despite her nerves, Caroline couldn't help but smile a little at that. "My mother is exceptionally good at cooking," she agreed.

"And you should come over for a meal sometime," Rhonda said from behind them, bustling into the kitchen. Caroline had known she'd come in since breakfast started to be served in thirty minutes. Rhonda was starting her usual routine of checking the orders that guests would have put in the night before and getting them plated as everyone came down. She sometimes let Caroline help with the cooking, but breakfast service was her favorite part of running the inn, and always had been. She was attached to handling that, as Caroline was with so many other parts of the inn. "I'd be happy to cook for you. Shelby, right? Now that you're working here, you're practically part of the family."

Shelby smiled, and Caroline cleared her throat. "Well, I should finish showing you around. Especially the dining room, since guests will be in there soon. We'll take the place settings and get them on the table."

It was clear that Shelby was excited to be at the inn, working in hospitality again, and she was taking to it wonderfully. But Caroline couldn't help correcting her. It felt like an impulse, from how Shelby set out the place settings, to how she arranged the welcome packets for the guests. She put the tourism pamphlets, inn information and menu in a different order, and Caroline quickly took the folder from her, reorganizing them. "The sheet with Wi-Fi passwords, meal and event times, and all of the other inn information goes in the back," she explained again. "Largest sheet to smallest. Then the tourism information, and then the menu in the very front, since it's the most aesthetic part of it."

She *knew* she was being nitpicky and set in her ways. But she had always had a very certain way that she liked things done, cultivated over years of running the inn full-time. It didn't help her mood that Margo was puttering around in the kitchen, clearly dead-set on making lunch for herself and Nora today of all days. Margo always made a huge mess when she cooked, using too many dishes and spreading them out everywhere, and Caroline gave the kitchen a wide berth so that she didn't accidentally get irritated with her sister. She knew it wasn't Margo's fault, she just wished her sister had picked any other day to decide to go all in on making lunch.

A little bit before lunchtime, Caroline came downstairs after showing Shelby how to make the beds and clean the guest rooms. She'd given Shelby a checklist, hovering the whole time, and Shelby had done all of the tasks well, but she hadn't been able to help redoing the beds. They just hadn't been quite the way she liked them to look, the way Rhonda had always taught her to fix them.

Through it all, Shelby had been cheerful and patient, redoing everything that Caroline had asked her to, and making notes of all the things that Caroline had corrected her on. It was clear that she very much wanted to keep the job, and was eager to learn, which made Caroline feel a little guilty that she was being so hard on her.

"Shelby, why don't you take a break for lunch with me," Rhonda said when they came back downstairs. "I have herbed chicken wraps for us, and some of that butternut squash soup that Margo is taking leftovers from for lunch too. Caroline, as much as I'd love to have you join us, why don't you go down and fix lunch for Rhett and Toby? Jay will be coming in with his friends too, I bet. You could use some time at home after the long morning."

Caroline started to protest, and her mother linked her elbow through hers, steering Caroline away for a moment.

"I know you mean well," Rhonda murmured. "But I think Shelby could use a little break from all the hovering, and I'd like to get to know her better. And I think you could use a break too," she added firmly. "Get some time to breathe at home. We can handle everything here for now."

Caroline wanted to argue, but she could tell that her mother wasn't going to let her get away with not taking a break. "Okay," she agreed reluctantly, glancing once more at Shelby before heading out of the backdoor and down to her small cottage further back on the property.

Rhett had been watching Toby all morning, and she heard her son's happy coo as soon as she walked into the house. She took off her boots and coat, hearing Rhett call a greeting from the living room, and walked into the warm space to see him on the floor with Toby, pushing a large wooden car back and forth.

"You're so good with him," she said with a smile, and Rhett grinned.

"I didn't have as much time with Jay when he was little. The fire station in Cleveland took up a lot more of my time. I'm glad I get to do all of this with Toby." He pushed the car again, much to the little boy's glee, and then scooped him up to bring him to Caroline. "How did it go today?"

Caroline shrugged, biting her lip. "She's eager to learn," she said neutrally, scooping Toby into her arms and kissing the top of his head as she walked into the kitchen to see what they had for lunch. She'd made a hot bacon and broccoli salad the night before and venison burgers, and she thought that she had some left over. She had been too stressed out all morning to be very hungry, and she thought that one of her favorite meals might help.

"Is she still there?" Rhett asked, taking Toby back

after Caroline had snuggled him for a minute, so that she could make lunch.

"Yes." Caroline took the containers with the leftovers out, divvying them up onto plates to reheat, and looking for the bag of buns she'd gotten from the local bakery. "Mom wanted to eat lunch with her and get to know her a little better. And Margo is tearing up the kitchen trying to make sandwiches for herself and Nora for their meeting to work on wedding planning, so it was all extra chaotic today. Mom insisted I come down here and see you guys for a little while, and make lunch for you and Jay."

"I wouldn't have minded making lunch. But I'm happy to see you for a bit. That's the perk of working for yourself, isn't it?" Rhett reminded her, and Caroline blew out a sharp breath, giving him a pointed look. He knew very well that working for herself had only ever meant that she had absolutely no work-life balance. Hiring Shelby was supposed to change that, but right now the thought of letting go enough to actually have that balance made her feel so alarmed that she didn't know if it was possible.

Just then, Jay burst in, preventing her from going further down that train of thought. He had two of his friends with him, excitedly asking if they could stay for lunch, and Caroline agreed, since there were enough venison burgers for all. Her mind immediately calmed as she started to go through the motions of making lunch for five, and she knew that it was because she had something to keep her busy.

She couldn't always be busy though. She needed time for herself, she knew. She needed to be able to relax, to read a book, and make herself her favorite candy cane tea, and spend time with her family. Needing to keep her hands busy at all times was something she'd been working on all her life, and it was long past time for her to really put effort into conquering it.

With a long sigh, she put together the plates of food, bringing the burgers and broccoli salad to the table. She had a distinct sense of satisfaction as she watched the three pre-teen boys tear into the salad as well as the burgers. It was hard to get them to eat their vegetables, and it felt like proof that she'd mastered her mother's recipe.

"This is delicious," Rhett told her, and Caroline smiled, holding Toby with one arm as she dug into her own lunch with the other.

The kitchen smelled warmly of food and the warmth of people gathered together, the faint fir smell of the Christmas tree from the living room and the leftover woodsmoke from the fireplace the night before, and she felt her shoulders relax slightly. Staying busy usually calmed her mind, but her family did too, and having Shelby at the inn would give her more time with them. It really wasn't something she could argue *wasn't* good for her, and for everyone else who really mattered to her.

Still, when lunch was finished and Jay and his friends had gone back out, she couldn't resist going back up to the inn after a short break with Rhett and Toby. She'd managed to stay home until about four-thirty, but it was getting close to when Shelby would be leaving, and she couldn't stop herself from giving Rhett a quick kiss and heading back up the hill to check on how things were going.

She found Shelby in the guests' dining room, putting out the place settings for the morning.

"I thought I'd get a jump on these," she said. "And everything is prepped for the morning. I double checked to make sure all the ingredients your mother needs are in the fridge, got the muffin baskets set out, and checked to make sure there's enough coffee, tea and cocoa. One of the guests specifically requested cinnamon oat milk creamer for their coffee, but that's already been picked up, and it's in the refrigerator."

Caroline personally didn't like to set out the

place settings until the morning. She thought it felt more fresh. But Rhonda walked in just then, a bright smile on her face, and she knew she shouldn't criticize Shelby again. There were plenty of times when Rhonda got the table set the night before. There was nothing wrong with it, and it saved time in the morning. It just wasn't Caroline's preferred way.

But she was going to have to let go of some of those habits, and she knew it.

"I would say the first day was a success," Rhonda said cheerily, and Shelby smiled in agreement.

"I had a wonderful time," she said. "I can't wait to be back. It hardly feels like a job at all, really."

Caroline couldn't deny that it had been a successful day. Shelby had happily done everything asked of her, and Caroline couldn't really find fault with any of it. Still, she couldn't help noticing that Shelby had grabbed the plain green placemats for the table settings, instead of the ones with the holly embroidery on the edges, and she couldn't force herself to keep quiet.

"Just one thing," she said quickly. "The placemats should be the holly ones. They're in the linen closet. If you can swap those out, that would be great. We start using them by this point in the season."

Shelby grinned. "Of course," she said easily. "Happy to do that. I'll remember to use those next time."

There really wasn't anything else that Caroline *needed* to do, beyond going back and double-checking everything as she was wont to do. The cookies and mulled wine had already been prepared for the social hour for the guests, the rooms were done up, and everything was set up for breakfast the next day. Her parents had their leftovers from the meal prep that Caroline had helped Rhonda do earlier in the week, and the inn itself was spotless. Even with looking over Shelby's shoulder as she'd done everything, having the extra pair of hands had helped everything move much more quickly.

Other than feeding the animals, which she could do on her way out, she was perfectly fine to go home for the evening.

She knew she should be relieved. For the first time in recent memory, her evening was open, with plenty of time to do her own house chores, get dinner in the oven, and still spend time with her family. But as she checked the food and water for the chickens and goats, double-checked the gates, and then headed back down the hill to her cottage, she felt strangely out of sorts.

The feeling persisted as she went upstairs to shower and change. Rhett walked into the bedroom just as she was pulling on her favorite sweatshirt with a print of two dachshunds in kilts on it, and she saw him notice the look on her face immediately.

"What's wrong?" Rhett asked, looking at her with kind concern. "I thought today went well? And you're home so much earlier than usual. I'm very happy about that," he added with a grin.

Caroline let out a sigh, chewing on her lower lip. "I feel like I'm neglecting the inn," she admitted. "Everything is done that needs to be, but someone else did it. I feel like someone is going to notice that something is out of place, or forgotten, or it will just *feel* different to the guests. To Mom and Dad. It feels like I'm not doing as much as I should."

Rhett slipped his arms around her, holding her close. "Hiring Shelby shows that you're doing the exact opposite of neglecting it," he said firmly. "It shows you're doing what any good business owner should—delegating, so that things don't get neglected and forgotten. You can't do it all."

"I always have though." Caroline sighed, leaning

into him. "And it feels so strange letting anyone else help."

"You'll see." He kissed the side of her head. "Having a healthier balance and more time to spend with your family will be worth it."

She knew he was right. But still, she knew it would take some time to get used to things being different.

Now, at least, she had more of it.

CHAPTER TWELVE

Nora let out a deep breath of relief as she put Madison down for her nap the next afternoon, and was met with blissful silence as she walked out a few minutes later, except for the soft sound of the crib mobile behind her as she closed the door.

Last night, there had been a few episodes of barking, which she and Aiden had mitigated by finally giving in and moving Chessie's bed into their room, where she could be close to them. *That* had resulted in being woken up just before their alarm by the puppy in between them, happily licking Aiden's face. She was, apparently, a very big fan of the scent of his aftershave.

He'd taken it in good stride though, and Chessie had been calm for most of the morning. Nora had been able to get breakfast ready for herself and Aiden—thawed-out sausage and egg biscuits, but homemade, and very good—and get Madison to eat some yogurt before Chessie had demanded to go outside. They'd gone for a walk, tiring both Madison and the puppy out, and now Madison was sleeping soundly.

Maybe she had gotten both child *and* puppy parenting down, after all.

The house wasn't as tidy as normal, but it wasn't terrible. There were both Madison and Chessie's toys to pick up now, but she could manage, and the dishes needed to be done, but only from this morning. Right now, her most pressing task was the laundry, since Aiden had a project to work on that weekend and would need his work clothes to be clean.

For all the craziness, there was a certain satisfaction in all of it that she was surprised she enjoyed as much as she did. She hadn't gone back to event planning full-time yet, choosing to put most of her focus into Margo's wedding, with just one other baby shower coming up in January. The rest of the time, she kept house and took care of Madison, and now Chessie as well, and she loved it so much more than she would ever have believed she could. When she'd lived in Boston, she'd wondered if she would go crazy being away from work long enough to go on maternity leave. But now she was just happy that she had the opportunity to stay at home with Madison, and not miss a single minute.

Life really did work out the way it was supposed to, she reflected as she went down to get the clean laundry out of the dryer, tossing another load in. She set the basket on the floor in the living room, thinking that she would fold those clothes in a bit, and maybe watch something on TV while she did. Madison wouldn't be awake for a little while, and she could grab a few moments just to herself.

Aiden had picked up a new chew toy for Chessie on the way home last night, a puzzle toy that she could hide small treats in, and she gave that to Chessie as she walked into the kitchen. Surely, she thought, that would keep the puppy busy while she made lunch. Lunch wouldn't take her long anyway. She had more of the leftover soup that Rhonda had sent her home with yesterday, as well as local Swiss cheese to make grilled cheese sandwiches with, and leftover baked apples from dessert last night.

Altogether, she thought, it would be a quick and cozy lunch, and then she could get started on the remainder of the chores while the house was still quiet.

She turned on a Christmas radio station on a low volume while she started to work, feeling once again that things were mostly under control. The to-do list felt manageable, Madison was asleep, and Chessie was contentedly chewing. She puttered around the kitchen, assembling sandwiches while the soup reheated, only to hear a sudden clatter from the living room and the sound of nails scratching on wood.

Nora dropped the wooden spoon she'd been holding, turning off the stove and rushing out to the living room. She was greeted by the sight of the laundry basket overturned in the middle of the room, clothes strewn everywhere, out past the boundaries of the living room. It was fairly clear who the culprit was—she could see that Chessie's chew toy was abandoned, and there was no sign of the puppy.

"Chessie!" She called out for the dog as she righted the laundry basket, gathering up the clothes closest to it as she looked for her. "Chessie!"

A moment later, the puppy came running out of the bathroom, a shirt in her mouth, looking endlessly pleased with herself. She tossed her head, ears flopping, and Nora let out a sigh, shaking her head as well.

It definitely seemed that she had underestimated what, exactly, taking on a puppy would entail.

* * *

That morning, Spencer had called Margo and asked if she would meet him for lunch at Rockridge Grill in between his appointments, and she'd been excited to meet up. Even though they'd just had their date night out at Marie's the night before, she'd already missed him. She was excited to spend a half-hour with him over lunch, and even more excited for when, very soon, she would get to see him every single day.

But she also couldn't get the misplaced rings off of her mind. She hadn't been able to find them, even though she'd quite literally torn her bedroom apart looking again, and she couldn't stop thinking about it. Where on earth had she put them? It seemed like there were a very limited number of places that they could be, and she also thought that she had already exhausted them all. But apparently, she hadn't, because they still hadn't turned up.

"How did the meeting with Nora for the

wedding planning go?" Spencer asked as the waitress brought them their lunch—a turkey, apple, and local cheddar sandwich for him with a side of tomato soup, and a winter salad for Margo, with shredded turkey and cranberries, along with a sweet maple dressing. "We didn't talk about it over dinner last night."

"We got too excited talking about the honeymoon."

She smiled, thinking of the plans they'd discussed for outings in the Galapagos, and all the pictures she'd brought to show Spencer over dinner. He'd been excited by the beautiful water and the promise of animal sightings, and she'd showed him the treehouse that they were staying in, which had plenty of amenities. It wasn't nearly as close to roughing it as he'd been worried that it might be.

"The plans are going well," she added. "I think we're nearly just about done. It's just going over the finer details now, really."

Spencer smiled, taking a bite of his sandwich.

"Work has been insane lately. With that other clinic closing, we've had twice the number of patients. And while I'm so glad that I'm available to help, getting all of the medical records transferred over and working with insurance has been a nightmare. I was surprised that I even got a chance to make it to lunch today." He chuckled. "I'm not much of an event planner, but working on wedding planning sounds so much less stressful. I wouldn't mind swapping places with you for a day."

"You might be surprised." Margo thought wryly of just how stressful it had become, ever since she'd discovered the rings were missing. Spencer had no idea. "I really haven't had much of a hand in all the organization. Nora has handled that beautifully. I've just picked from what she's given me options for, and offered up a few ideas here and there."

"I'm sure it's going to be perfect," Spencer said. "You said everything that's been ordered has all come in, right?"

Margo nodded. That much, at least was true. It *had* all been delivered to Sugar Maple, she just couldn't remember where she'd misplaced one very specific, very important thing. Or two, rather. "I've stored a lot of it in my office at *The Gazette*," she said with a laugh. "Nora took some of it to her house as well, but with the new puppy, she didn't want too many things laying around that Chessie could get into. It's not as if we can rush order anything if it got damaged."

Spencer laughed. "That's probably for the best.

How is your sister handling a puppy *and* a baby anyway?"

"With a lot of patience," Margo said, laughing as well. "I think she's in a little over her head. I don't think she realized just how much of a handful Chessie would be. But Madison loves her, and Nora is determined to keep trying."

"Maybe we should get a dog," Spencer said thoughtfully. "What kind would you want?"

"A corgi," Margo said immediately. "Small enough to cuddle on the couch with, big enough to go on hikes. What about you?" she asked curiously. This was a topic they hadn't discussed before, and she felt a little flutter of excitement. Before moving home to Evergreen Hollow, she'd never been at her apartment long enough to have a pet. She'd always been jet-setting to one place or another, too often to even have a fish tank. But now, she could get a puppy. She and Spencer could, and the thought of that new addition to their future made her feel more than a little eager.

"I think I'd want a husky," Spencer said. "Perfect for the snow, good for walks, like you said. A bit large for couch snuggles, but we could always get a larger couch." He smiled, and Margo returned it, thinking of the white-painted farmhouse that she would be moving into after the wedding. Spencer had inherited it from his father, and she couldn't wait to make it theirs.

"They're very high energy," she considered. "But I do go out hiking a lot. And even if you were busy, I have a good bit of extra time."

"I was thinking a husky would be just the thing to keep you safe on those hikes," Spencer said with a smile. "But we have plenty of time to talk about it."

"I'll have to get all moved in before we can even think about bringing a puppy home," Margo agreed, and she saw Spencer's face light up, his hand sliding across the table to wrap around hers.

"I'm so excited to marry you," he told her. "I can't wait for our wedding day. And I'm so grateful that you came back to Evergreen Hollow."

He squeezed her hand as he said it, and Margo's eyes abruptly filled with tears. It seemed like the sweetest thing he'd ever said to her in that moment, coming from a man who had said so many sweet and romantic things. She felt the same way. But at that moment, she couldn't help but think of the fact that she couldn't find their wedding rings. The very rings that she'd had specially engraved to represent just how ready she was to stay in Evergreen Hollow, and forever be Spencer's wife.

She couldn't help but feel that it was yet another moment where Spencer was all in, ready and there for her without doubt, and she'd managed to fall short again. She knew he didn't feel that way, and that the absence of the rings wasn't anything other than just a moment of forgetfulness, that she would fix just as soon as she found them.

But she still had to wipe away the tears, worried that she wouldn't be able to find them in the end.

"Are you all right?" Spencer asked, concerned, and Margo nodded.

"I'm just so happy," she said, smiling at him. And it was the truth. She was happy, happier than she could have ever imagined to be marrying him and starting their life together. And hearing him say how excited he was only made her feel even more happy.

She was just worried that she might have messed up one of the only things that had been hers to handle in all of this wedding planning.

Spencer leaned over, giving her a kiss, and setting some cash on the table to cover their lunch. "I need to go," he said, squeezing her hand once more. "The clinic is probably going to be overflowing when I get back."

As soon as he had left, she grabbed her phone, typing out a frantic message to Nora.

MARGO: We need to double our efforts to find the rings. Triple them. I *have* to figure out where they are.

NORA: Any ideas? We already looked everywhere at the inn.

MARGO: We'll start with my office at *The Gazette*. Maybe they're still where the decorations are stashed.

NORA: Okay. I'll meet you there. Sunday?

MARGO: Sunday it is. We have to find them.

CHAPTER THIRTEEN

That afternoon, once she'd eaten lunch with Jay and he'd gone back out to play with his friends, Caroline bundled Toby up to go for a walk with him in his stroller. Rhonda had insisted that since Shelby was doing so well, Caroline should work a half-day, and just go home and spend time with Toby after lunch. She'd pointed out that anything left to do, she could double-check to make sure that Shelby had done correctly, and so far, everything had been just fine, with no mishaps.

Which was technically true, Caroline had to admit. Shelby hadn't made any real mistakes, and she'd picked up on the rhythms of the inn quickly. She was hardworking, always cheerful, and quick to step in when something needed to be done. There really wasn't anything else that Caroline could ask for out of an employee—other than to not have one, and for her to have the time and possibly an extension of herself to just do it all the way she knew she liked to have it done.

But she had to admit that she couldn't remember the last time she'd been able to just go for a walk during the day. She'd missed it, and even more so now that she could take Toby out walking with her in his stroller. Nora often talked about doing the same with Madison, and Caroline could remember on any number of occasions thinking longingly of how nice that sounded.

Now, she thought, she could do it—and she was just thinking about how she should be at the inn working instead.

She took a deep breath, intentionally clearing her head of the worries about the inn. She got Toby's beanie and mittens on, tucking him in the blankets in his stroller, and started down the path that would take her around the inn and out to the main street. She thought she would take a walk down to The Mellow Mug, get a coffee, and come back. A peppermint mocha sounded wonderful, and even with the extra time, she still had plenty to catch up on at home. The caffeine would be a good boost.

The weather was beautiful, if cold, the sky bright and sunny as they walked, sparkling off of the snow. She smiled to herself, thinking of the days when she'd first met Rhett, when she'd gone on walks like this and found an abandoned journal tucked by her favorite tree, and started writing to the person it had belonged to. She hadn't known it was Rhett who had lost the journal until long after she'd already started to like him far more than she'd thought she should, back then.

But as it turned out, she'd liked him exactly the right amount. He'd liked her too. And they'd fallen in love—something she'd given up on, and now she had all of this. Two children, a home of her own, and a husband she adored and who adored her in return.

And now she finally had time to relax and live in the moment. To enjoy everything she'd worked so hard for and been so fortunate to have.

She felt herself doing exactly that as she walked to The Mellow Mug, enjoying the scenery and the crisp air. The shop was nearly empty when she got there, and Melanie greeted her cheerfully.

"An Americano?" she asked, and Caroline shook her head.

"I'll do a peppermint mocha, I think. And some

of that peppermint decaf loose-leaf tea that you sell too?"

She had plans to read a book by the fire before bed that evening, and make her favorite candy cane tea treat. It brought back fond memories of when she'd made a nightly habit of exactly that in her bedroom upstairs at the inn, when she'd treated herself to an electric fireplace for the room.

A fireplace that had ended up being wired poorly, and eventually led to her meeting her handsome fireman.

"Coming right up." Melanie rang up the order and started the coffee. A few minutes later, Caroline had a sachet of the loose-leaf tea and a to-go mug of coffee, and she was ready to start the walk back home.

She felt thoroughly refreshed by the relaxation and the walk. She honestly thought she might have felt energized even without the jolt of caffeine. As she headed back, she thought she finally had the energy to dig out the lawn ornaments that she usually would have put up by now in front of the inn.

She'd been too busy and overwhelmed to get to it before today, but that afternoon felt like the perfect time. And Rhonda would be pleased; Caroline knew her mother liked to have it all done right after Thanksgiving. The last few years, Caroline had made sure to do the same. Rhonda hadn't said anything about it, probably, Caroline thought, because she knew how busy Caroline had been, but she'd worried that her mother was disappointed.

But after today, all of that would be fixed.

Energized and ready to tackle that one last task before heading back home for good that evening, she took Toby back to the cottage, where Jay was in the living room doing his homework in front of the fire.

"Can you keep an eye on Toby until your dad gets home?" she asked, unbundling Toby from his small fleece coat and beanie. "I'm going to run back up to the inn and finish some decorating for your grandma. I'll be back in a couple of hours, but I think your dad will be home before then, even."

"Sure thing." Jay smiled, scooting aside as Caroline laid Toby down on his mat, getting out a handful of toys. "Here, we'll play with cars in between me doing my homework."

He pushed the brightly colored wooden cars that Toby loved in a circle, mimicking the voices from the animated movie. Toby giggled happily, waving his fists, and Caroline smiled, a flood of happiness filling her chest.

She paused for a moment, rather than rushing out, taking the time to appreciate it. When she'd found out that she was pregnant last Christmas, she'd worried about how Jay would feel. She'd worried he might feel replaced, or that he wasn't getting the attention he needed. But instead, he'd become the best big brother she could have imagined. He loved Toby, and few things made her as happy as watching them together.

It really was everything she could have hoped for.

"I'll be back before dinner," she promised again, grabbing her gloves and heading out. She trooped up the hill to the inn, circling around to the front to check on the lights that were already out, planning to go inside right after and collect the boxes of lawn ornaments to put out.

But as she rounded the corner, she stopped short, shocked.

All of the remaining lawn ornaments and decorations were already out. The garlands were wrapped around the porch, the new holiday cushions on the porch chairs, the lighted deer, the snowman, and the rustic Christmas Mistletoe Inn sign all out in their usual places—although, to her eye, slightly off from how she usually arranged them. But it was all lovely... and all already done.

Rhonda emerged from the front door a moment later with a new sleigh-shaped doormat. She saw Caroline standing in the front yard and beamed, motioning excitedly for Caroline to come up the stairs.

"What do you think?" She gestured to the yard. "We got it all done for you. Shelby did most of it, honestly, since it's harder for me to be out in the snow with my hip lugging things around these days. But I oversaw it. Isn't it great?"

Caroline felt as if her mouth might drop open. "I—this has always been my job," she stammered, trying to fight back the surge of emotion that threatened to make her eyes well up with tears. "I was going to take care of it. I just—"

Rhonda looped her arm through Caroline's, tugging her daughter to the edge of the porch to overlook the now thoroughly decorated yard. "I know," she said calmly. "But Shelby was very efficient getting through all her afternoon tasks today. She was looking for something to do, and you were getting to enjoy your afternoon for once. Instead of leaving something on your plate, Shelby thought she could help out, and I was inclined to agree. And it looks great. Now you don't need to worry about it."

Caroline bit her lip, taking in all of it. She couldn't deny that it did look good, as good as her work usually did. And she had been putting it off, and now she didn't need to any longer. But she felt her heart sink. This was the first year she hadn't had any hand in helping to put them out. It didn't mean anything, but it *felt* like it did.

Just that moment, Jay came skidding around the front of the inn, dragging his sleigh. "Dad came home early and has Toby!" he called out. "I'm going to get in one more round of sledding with my friends before it gets dark. Dad said it's okay." He looked around, taking in his surroundings quickly. "Man, the ornaments look cool!"

Without another word, he darted off, and Caroline pressed her hand to her mouth, unsure of whether she wanted to laugh or cry.

She had so much more time now. She could delegate. There was someone who was apparently capable and trustworthy enough to hand tasks over to, so she could enjoy the benefits of being her own boss that she'd never been able to before.

There were so many possibilities that came with Shelby being a part of the inn. Trips she and Rhett could take with the kids, or alone. They'd never gone on vacations, because she didn't feel she could leave the inn. More date nights. More time just at home, enjoying it. Time to pick up one of the many hobbies she'd considered over the years and just really never was able to commit to.

She wished she could let go a little easier so that she could just be happy about that. She needed to let Shelby do her job, and be glad that she was there.

But it was more difficult than she could possibly have anticipated.

CHAPTER FOURTEEN

Sunday afternoon, Margo's office at *The Gazette* was a disastrous mess.

She and Nora had torn through every box and bag looking for the rings, all but dismantled her desk, and looked in every crevice of the room for the rings that they could possibly be in, all to no avail. Her desk was much cleaner now, and she'd gotten rid of a lot of unnecessary papers, but still no rings.

Margo plopped onto the floor next to a pile of decorations that she and Nora had taken out of their boxes, frustrated and anxious. She knew she could be disorganized and scatterbrained when it came to everything other than her job, but she'd never been *this* disorganized before. She lost track of unimportant things, or things like keys or sunglasses, or sometimes forgot appointments. But when something was *important*, like deadlines or getting the details right on a photo or especially something like her actual wedding rings, she'd always kept those things straight.

The wedding planning had been chaotic, but she hadn't thought she'd been that stressed out or distracted. But she must have been, because she could still swear she remembered putting the rings in her nightstand at home, and yet they weren't there. Or anywhere else in her bedroom, or her office, apparently.

Nora sat back from looking through the final box with a sigh, giving Margo an apologetic look. "They're not there."

"Don't look at me like that," Margo said, letting out a sigh of her own. "You have nothing to be sorry for. *I'm* sorry for dragging you out on a Sunday afternoon to look for *my* rings that I lost."

"If I were your event planner, I'd invoice you for it," Nora said cheekily. "But fortunately, I'm your sister. So of course I'm going to come help."

She glanced over at Chessie, who had finished the peanut butter in her Kong, and was now looking around for something else to occupy herself with. Margo knew she'd been hesitant to bring the puppy anywhere near the wedding decorations, but Rhonda was already watching Madison, and Aiden was working over the weekend to get repairs done for a neighbor before the next snow came in.

Margo handed her the other chew toy that Nora had brought, and Nora gave it to Chessie. The puppy considered it for a moment, looked around the room once more for other options, and then settled down to once again start gnawing.

"How's that going?" Margo asked, looking at the puppy, and Nora tipped her head to one side.

"Like having a baby times two," she said, without much irony. "Okay, it's not *quite* as involved as a baby. But I'm chasing both of them all of the time. Chessie can get into something just as quickly as Madison can, that's for sure. I need eyes in the back of my head. The barking has gotten a little better since we started letting her sleep in the bedroom. But now she wants to get in *our* bed, and wake us up by licking our faces. Which we put up with because it's better than her barking and waking up Madison."

"Spencer was just talking the last time we had lunch about getting a puppy." Margo smiled ruefully. "Maybe you should fill him in on the cons, since all he can see right now are pros. To be honest, I kind of like the idea too. He wants a husky, so I have a buddy for my hikes."

"That's a good idea," Nora said, glancing over at Chessie once more. "You could use a hiking buddy to keep an eye out for you. It could always run for help if you get in trouble again." She grinned at Margo, who rolled her eyes playfully.

"None of you are ever going to let that go, are you?"

"It happened *twice*. In the last two years. I wouldn't if I were Spencer either." Nora laughed. "You're accident-prone. But honestly, it's not the puppy that's hard. It's more the baby and puppy at the same time. But I'm determined to figure it out."

"Of course you are." Margo smiled fondly, looking over at Chessie as well. "I like that Spencer is so excited for our future. The wedding, getting a puppy together, all of it. And I can't wait for it all too. I just need to find the rings," she added, clicking her tongue against her teeth as she looked around the mess that their search had made of the office. "I can't think of where else they could be."

"Mentally retrace what you did the day that you picked them up," Nora suggests. "Step-by-step. Maybe that will help."

Margo frowned, trying to think.

"I was heading to work that morning, and Melanie was at the inn. She told me she'd heard the rings had been delivered, and she wanted to see them, so we both went to Sugar Maple to pick them up." She chewed on her lip, trying to replay the morning in her head. "I was in a little bit of a hurry because I was running late for work, but nothing too frantic. I knew Sabrina wouldn't care if I was late because of wedding stuff, and it's not as if I'm behind on any projects. If anything, I'm ahead of schedule. So it wasn't like I was all that stressed out—"

"Focus," Nora gently encouraged. "Step-by-step."

"Right." Margo rubbed her hands together, thinking. "Leon had the rings, and we spent some time looking at them. He said he had the other decorations too, so we ended up loading those all into the car so I could bring them with me. It was all super chaotic because Bethany was helping and she still had Chessie then, so Chessie was running around and all underfoot. I put the rings in my coat pocket. No, wait! Maybe I gave them to Melanie to hang onto. No, I'm sure I put them in my coat." She shook her head. "But maybe they were the last thing I took out. I remember setting them on the counter."

"But you're sure you took them with you?" Nora asked, and Margo nodded insistently.

"Yes, of course. I'm sure. At some point, I put them in my coat pocket. And then I dropped Melanie off, grabbed another coffee while I was there, and headed to the office. Sabrina stopped me to ask about my running late, and all the bags I was bringing in, and we talked about wedding stuff. And then I talked to you about coming to pick up decorations, and you said you'd make it as soon as you could, since you were getting Chessie from Bethany."

"And what about after that?" Nora prompted, and Margo blew out a long breath.

"I staged all the boxes and bags so they wouldn't look like a mess in here. And I put the ring boxes in my purse. Or maybe I zipped them up in my camera bag." She looked up at the ceiling, frustrated. "Wherever I put them, I *swear* I remember taking them home and putting them in my nightstand upstairs. But clearly I didn't, because we tore through my room looking." Margo's shoulders slump. "I feel more confused than ever now."

Nora frowned, and it was clear that she wasn't sure what to say. They seemed to have come to a dead end, and Margo covered her hands with her face.

"I wanted this to be such a great surprise! And now I've ruined everything." Her shoulders hunched forward, and Nora reached out, rubbing her sister's back.

"You haven't ruined everything," Nora said comfortingly. "The rings are just a symbol. A really sweet, special one, but still just a symbol. Spencer knows how much you love him with or without specially engraved rings. He would know even without the fancy wedding, or the ceremony, or any of it. All of that is just a way to make memories, Margo. To mark a special day and celebrate with *all* the people who love you. But it doesn't make Spencer know you love him any more or less than he does right now."

Margo looked up, sniffling slightly, her eyes damp. "Do you really think so?"

"Absolutely," Nora assured her. "It's in all the ways you've shown him, over two whole years. You didn't think you were going to stay in Evergreen Hollow, but you couldn't help but spend time with him, even though you thought you shouldn't let yourself fall for him. You found ways to make yourself more at home here, because you wanted to be happy enough to have a life here with him. You're having a big wedding because you know he's excited for it, even though I know you'd be just as happy getting married in the living room of the inn and then going out to dinner and calling it a day. All of those things matter, Margo. And those are just the *serious* reasons," she added.

Margo frowned, but the worry was starting to leave her expression, and she could feel her tension easing. "What do you mean, the *serious* reasons?" she asked, laughing a little.

"I mean that there are smaller ones too." Nora leaned back against the wall, smiling. "There's the fact that you bought yourself a planner to try to get more organized, because you know Spencer is so busy, and you wanted to be able to help. Even though I also know that you never use it, because it's sitting on the corner of your desk right now with the sticker from the store still on it."

She grinned as she added, "And you've been trying like a maniac to get better at cooking and baking, because you think it's more domestic. Caroline said you even tried to *dust* the other day, even though she also said that all that happened was that there were streaks of dust on the mantle instead. You're not domestic or a homemaker, which is totally fine, and I don't think Spencer really cares. He's marrying you for *you*, not a checklist of a wife. But what matters is that you keep trying, because you want to be the best possible wife you can be for Spencer, and I know he sees that."

"I didn't even think about it like that," Margo said honestly. "I just know I wanted to be a good partner for him. And I want him to be happy. I want him to always be as happy about us being together as he is right now."

"Sometimes it might feel like things are rocky," Nora confided. "Mom gave me that advice, before Aiden and I got married. There will be things that test you. Babies and unexpected house repairs and bills and schedules—and puppies," she added with a laugh. "But as long as you work together as a team, that's all that matters. Definitely more than rings or cooking or planners. And I know Spencer feels the same way."

Margo smiled, feeling her worries ease. "I'm glad we had this ta—"

She was cut off by a sudden *thud*, and the rustling sound of something hard and glassy spilling out all over the wooden floor. Chessie let out a series of high-pitched, excited yips, and Margo looked to see that, bored with her chew toy, the puppy had overturned a box of decorative marbles intended to go in the vases at the wedding.

They were currently *everywhere,* spreading out over the entire office, rolling under furniture and Margo's desk and anywhere else that they could find a crack to slip through.

Margo let out a groan, and Nora laughed, pushing herself up from the floor to go and capture the rambunctious puppy. "What was that about wanting a dog?" she asked, but the question dissolved into more laughter as Chessie started to eagerly lick her face, squirming happily. It was clear that she didn't have the slightest idea of the inconvenience she'd caused.

"You hold her," Nora said, handing the wriggling puppy to Margo. "I'll start gathering up the marbles, so she doesn't try to eat any, and then we can trade off. And then," she added, "we'll think of where to look for your rings next."

The confidence in her voice made Margo feel slightly more hopeful that they would, in fact, uncover the mystery of the missing rings before the wedding. And if not, she thought as she held onto

Chessie, she felt reassured by what her sister had said.

Rings or no rings, Spencer loved her. Their wedding bands could be replaced, but that couldn't.

And in the end, that was all that really mattered.

CHAPTER FIFTEEN

Nora double-checked her grocery list, adding the ingredients for peppermint chocolate drop cookies to it as she glanced out to the living room where Chessie was, hopefully, still sleeping.

It had been a long day. Nora had planned to catch up on house chores during Madison's nap, and she'd been hopeful that it would be a success.

Madison was back to her usual sleep schedule, naps included, and the solution of keeping Chessie in her and Aiden's bedroom at night to sleep had solved the nighttime barking. It had definitely been an issue of separation anxiety. She was still waking Nora and Aiden up every morning, but she had at least started to adjust to their schedule, so she didn't usually jump up onto the bed until just before the alarm clocks went off. Aiden had joked that they might as well get rid of them, with Chessie around. She was every bit as good as one.

But today, Chessie had gotten bored of her array of chew toys, and had decided to attack a feather pillow on the couch. Nora had thought, so far, that the pillows were safe, but they had turned out to be the subject of Chessie's attention that afternoon. She'd torn it apart before Nora had caught her, and left feathers scattered all over the living room and beyond.

It had taken a long time to clean up. Well past the time when Madison had woken up from her nap, and then she'd been cranky, because Nora had been focused on cleaning up feathers instead of playing with her. She was sure that she hadn't gotten them all, and the only consolation had been that at least she'd accomplished the chore of sweeping while trying to gather them all up.

Madison had been too cranky and fussy to eat much of her lunch, and Nora had decided to make it up to her by going to the park. They'd gotten all bundled up, and she'd put Chessie on her leash, taking the opportunity to get them all some fresh air.

She figured that would get some of the puppy's boundless energy out, and cheer Madison up. A walk always did them both a lot of good.

It had been a gorgeous day too. There had been a heavy snow the day before, with enough time for the plows to come out and clear the paths, so what was left were sparkling big drifts. The park was covered in snow as well, but there was the large, open pavilion that was cleared out, with a small play area for the littler ones and heat lamps hanging from the roof, as well as a fireplace at the far end. It was remarkably cozy, and Nora had settled in with Madison, chasing her and Chessie around the play area until they were both suitably tired out.

It had been a fun afternoon, that was for sure. Nora always loved those afternoon outings with Madison, and it had been more than a little entertaining watching her chase Chessie around in endless circles, running after the balls and tumbling over each other. Chessie was a remarkably tolerant puppy, letting Madison grab handfuls of her fur and tug on her ears, and Nora couldn't deny that both the baby and the puppy seemed to have taken to each other since the moment they'd met.

The downside of the unplanned outing was that it had put her even further behind on her to-do list.

She hadn't gotten a chance to run to the general store yet for her dinner supplies, and it was already five in the evening. She was supposed to be starting dinner shortly, not still getting around to going shopping.

Chalking it up to the chaos that she'd told herself she was more than capable of managing, Nora bundled up Madison again, getting Chessie in her harness and leash, and loading everyone up in the car to drive to Sugar Maple. She knew that Aiden would be home late—winter projects often ran into the evenings, when he and Blake would bring out the floodlights and work well past dark. This time of year, any unexpected storm could throw off schedules by days or weeks, so when the weather was clear, he'd work as long as he could.

At least, she reflected, he wouldn't come home hungry to her running behind schedule. She'd expected to put aside leftovers for when he came in late, so it was really just herself and Madison that she needed to feed soon. That reminder made her feel better, as she drove through the snowy streets to Sugar Maple, enjoying the view. It was getting dark, and the Christmas lights all along Main Street glowed. It was brightly festive, and Nora felt her spirits lifting as she pulled into the parking lot and unloaded baby, dog, and stroller.

Bethany, to her surprise, was at the front counter when she walked in. "Leon had plans with some of his friends," she explained as Nora walked in, clearly catching the surprised look on her face. "I told him I'd close up so he could have more of the night off." She smiled as Nora walked over to the first shelf, looking over the array of dry goods there. "How are things going?"

"Oh, you know. Busy as always." Nora didn't want to let on just how frazzled she actually was, as she gathered up buns, ketchup, and a handful of potatoes. Burgers and fries for dinner sounded good, and while she briefly thought of just going and getting something to-go from Rockridge Grill, she decided to go ahead and cook. Being home and cooking something in the relaxing comfort of her own home would be simpler than another stop with both Madison and Chessie in tow, and she was hoping that after the excitement of the day, both of them would sleep for a good while.

"How is Chessie settling in so far?" There was a hint of a knowing smile in Bethany's voice, and Nora let out a small laugh.

"She's enjoying having the run of the house. How is the search for her owners going, by the way?" Nora asked, trying not to sound too interested. "Or have you found someone interested in adopting her yet?"

Bethany smiled. "No, I don't think her owners are anywhere to be found. They're definitely not in Evergreen Hollow, and she wasn't chipped. I've done all I can in that regard. But as far as adoption—" She glanced to where Chessie was curled up in Madison's stroller next to her, both baby and puppy sound asleep. "I think she's already found her forever home."

Nora pursed her lips to one side, lifting one shoulder. "She looks calm and peaceful now, but what you're seeing is definitely *not* how it is most of the time." She emphasized it as she spoke, keeping her voice low so as not to wake either Madison or Chessie. "I love Chessie, for sure, but it's been absolute chaos. I definitely underestimated the challenge."

Bethany smiled indulgently as Nora brought some of her purchases to the counter, leaving the stroller for a moment as she went over to the case where the meats were kept to pick out a package of ground beef.

"I don't know," she said slowly, her tone sing-song as she looked at the sleeping Madison and Chessie curled up together. "I don't think there's anything cuter than a little kid with a baby animal. That's the most adorable combination anyone could possibly come up with. Plus, the two of them have really taken to one another. And it'll be good for Madison, as she gets older."

Nora plopped the package of beef onto the counter next to her other groceries. "What do you mean by that?"

"Well..." Bethany started to ring it all up, her gaze still drifting over to the stroller with an expression that said she found the scene cute beyond words. "It's good for children to have a bit of responsibility as they grow up. A dog is an excellent way to teach that. And a companion is a good thing too. Madison and Chessie will both grow up together, and they'll always be inseparable. As Madison starts to walk and run around, Chessie will look out for her. It's the perfect partnership. *And*," she added with a flourish, reaching for a paper bag, "having to share the attention with someone else is good practice for Madison, in case you and Aiden decide to grow your family with a sibling or two for her."

Nora smiled, but she groaned inwardly, thinking that Bethany must have heard Aiden's comment about wanting a second baby that night when they stopped in front of the house. It felt like only a few days ago that she'd felt like superwoman, sure that she could handle a half-dozen kids if that's what she and Aiden decided on, no problem.

She'd thought that a second baby would be a breeze, and that a puppy would be even easier. Looking back, she felt the irony of the fact that she had been the one to convince Aiden that fostering Chessie was a great idea.

But she hadn't thought it would be permanent. And it *had* been good for Madison. The bond between her daughter and the puppy was clear, and she thought it had been good for Madison's mood overall, even if their routines had been upended.

That was the thing though, as she dodged Bethany's efforts to say for sure whether or not they would be keeping Chessie, and told her goodnight, taking the groceries out to the car. She'd had a carefully established routine, one that she and Aiden had worked hard to get right. They'd worked it out together, and she'd been very proud of how well they'd cracked the code of parenting.

Now it had been shaken. And it was making her second-guess if expanding beyond just having Madison was really the best idea. Maybe once they'd gotten that routine down, they should have stuck with it.

Just as she climbed into the car and started it, waiting for it to heat up before leaving, her phone buzzed. She saw that it was Aiden, and answered, rubbing her chilly hands over her jeans.

"Hey there," she said with a smile. "Everything all right?"

"Of course. I just realized that I didn't bring my laptop charger with me today. Do you know where it might be? It should have been on my desk with the rest of my things when I packed up this morning, and I guess it wasn't. My work computer is dead, and I need to pull up some blueprints for this house that Blake and I are repairing."

Nora grimaced. She was pretty sure she knew where that charger *might* be. "I haven't seen it," she said, drumming her fingers against the steering wheel. "But I would check in the most unlikely of places that are Chessie-sized."

Aiden chuckled. "You're probably right. I'll see if I can send them to Blake, maybe he can pull them up. Don't worry about it. I'll see you tonight."

"I'll look for the charger when I get home too," she promised.

"If you have time. Love you."

"Love you too." Nora hung up, glancing back at Chessie as she put the car in gear, who was sitting up in the backseat panting. The puppy was adorable, that much was undeniable. But Nora was also at her wit's end.

She couldn't even keep her own house in order, anymore.

CHAPTER SIXTEEN

Caroline rolled over onto her back in the middle of her soft, king-sized bed, stretching lazily as she yawned, just beginning to wake up. She felt warm and cozy, deliciously relaxed. Honestly, she thought drowsily, she felt more well-rested than she could remember feeling in a long time. She felt as if she'd gotten to sleep forever—

She sat bolt upright in the bed, blinking away the last bits of sleep as she looked over frantically at her alarm clock. She felt that way because she *had* slept forever. Or, rather, she'd slept until eight in the morning, which was basically the same thing, considering the fact that she typically got up at six. She had definitely overslept, and she craned to hear any sounds of Toby fussing or crying from his nursery.

But the house was entirely peaceful and quiet, not a sound to be heard.

She threw the covers back, shoving her feet into her slippers and padding down the stairs. There were no sounds from anyone, and she peeked into Toby's nursery to see that the crib was empty and neatly made up. Jay's room was the same, and she wondered if Rhett had taken them somewhere. He was supposed to work at the fire station this morning, but she wouldn't have put it past him to do an impromptu "take your kids to work" day, if only because he'd been nudging her more and more to take time for herself since Shelby had started work at the inn.

She absolutely could see him sweeping the boys away for a day and turning her alarm clock off to get her to do just that.

Walking into the kitchen, however, she saw a note on the counter. It was scribbled in Jay's hasty handwriting, and she couldn't help but smile as soon as she saw it.

Took Toby over to the inn. Having breakfast with Grandma. See you around.

• J

There was a hastily drawn heart at the bottom of it, and Caroline folded the note up, tucking it into the pocket of her robe with the intent to keep it. She quickly went back upstairs, throwing on a pair of jeans and a flannel and shoving her feet into her boots, before hurrying outside and up the hill to the inn. She knew everything would be fine, but she felt the urge to see for herself. Plus, she couldn't remember the last time she hadn't already been at the inn by this time in the morning. It felt strange to still be at home with it quiet and empty, and know that others were taking care of what she usually handled.

She walked up to the front door—once again noticing the lawn ornaments all set out—and knocked the snow off of her boots, slipping out of her jacket and gloves before heading into the living room, finding her little family happily assembled there.

Toby was in his high chair, being fed soft sweet potatoes by Jay, who was intermittently taking bites out of a peppermint chocolate muffin himself. Rhonda was sitting contentedly next to Jay on the couch, a mug of coffee next to her as she knitted what looked like a candy-cane striped beanie, the fire crackling merrily in front of her. And through the doorway that led to the kitchen, Caroline caught a glimpse of Shelby moving about.

Caroline swallowed hard, looking at each of them. It was a perfect, cozy family picture, and she knew Jay had done a sweet thing, bringing Toby up to the inn so that she could sleep in without interruption. She'd had a morning all to herself, and she had to admit that it had been sorely needed. She felt more refreshed than she had in a long time.

But she couldn't shake the flicker of uneasiness that she felt at everything running so smoothly, even though she hadn't even been up to the inn yet that morning.

"I'm just going to go grab some coffee and something to eat," she told Rhonda, who had set her knitting down for a moment. "I'll be right back. Thanks for keeping an eye on them."

"I hardly needed to do anything at all," Rhonda said with a smile. "Jay is a very capable big brother."

"Oh, I know he is." Caroline flashed a grateful smile at Jay, who beamed back at her, airplaning another spoonful of sweet potatoes into Toby's open, smiling mouth.

Shelby was at the counter when Caroline walked

in, dicing up potatoes. Caroline hesitated, seeing the ingredients spread out for what was undoubtedly the meals for guests who had requested lunch in addition to the included breakfast while staying at the inn.

"You didn't need to do that," Caroline said quickly. "I usually handle all the lunch prep after breakfast. It's a lot of work, and a lot of the guests have special requests or accommodations—"

"It's no trouble at all," Shelby said with a confident wave of her hand, smiling. "I've got it all under control. Your kids came up a little while ago, and Jay told your mother that you were getting to sleep in. I figured if I handled all of this, it would give you some more time to spend with them." She smiled conspiratorially, dropping the potatoes into a bowl. "Jay mentioned something about sled races happening at eleven this morning. He seemed very excited about it all. It sounds like it's a pretty big deal, to be honest. I had no idea the kids here took sledding so seriously."

She grinned, heading over to put the potatoes in a pot of boiling water, and Caroline heard Jay speak up abruptly from behind her. Apparently, he'd walked in on the end of that conversation.

"It's a relay-style sled race," he told her excitedly,

bouncing up and down on his toes in the doorway as Caroline turned around to look at him. His eyes were sparkling, and it was clear that he was every bit as excited as Shelby had said that he was. "My friends have a team! They've been badgering me to be on it with them, so I told them I would be. We could all go," he added. "Dad said he has to work today and couldn't get out of it, but you and Toby could be there!"

His excitement was palpable, and as much as she still felt the urge to be at the inn and work, as she always did, Caroline couldn't tell him no. This was the point of hiring Shelby, after all—so that she'd have time to do things like this. More time to appreciate the moments with her family that wouldn't be around forever. And she wanted to. She just had to figure out how to convince herself that it wasn't selfish.

She smiled at him. "Of course we can go. Let's get Toby and head back to the house. I want to shower and get him bundled up for the trip. And then we'll head out, okay? I wouldn't miss it."

Jay nodded eagerly, and Caroline went to grab herself a muffin and pour some coffee, watching as he tore out of the kitchen and back to the living room to clean up the remains of his and Toby's breakfast.

A few minutes later, they were all trooping back to the cottage, Rhonda and Shelby's assurances that the inn was well in hand ringing in Caroline's ears. She was excited for her day with her kids, but she couldn't help the heavy feeling in her chest that she wasn't actually needed at the inn. She'd spent so many years pouring herself into it, and now it seemed that it was chugging along just fine without her.

She wasn't entirely sure what to make of that. But she was determined not to let it get in the way of Jay's excitement. He *had* been really into sledding so far over the winter, going out nonstop and talking about it every day, and she hadn't seen him sled with his friends more than once. She definitely hadn't gotten to see him do anything like race. This was a definite opportunity for family time that she didn't want to miss.

Quickly, she jumped in the shower while Jay got ready, and then bundled up in jeans and a thick wool crew sweater, her favorite heavy jacket over it. She tugged on a beanie, and went to get Toby, wrapping him up in little fleece sweatpants and a sweater with a warm hoodie over it that had elephant ears on the hood. He cooed and waved his fists as she dressed him, always a happy baby, especially when it seemed like they were getting ready to go somewhere.

Ten or so minutes later, they were headed out. She got Toby buckled into the car seat as Jay clambered into the front, and she took them to The Mellow Mug first, so that she could get a hot drink to sip on while they were out in the cold.

"Can I get a peppermint hot chocolate?" Jay asked, and Caroline knew he was already bursting with energy without the extra sugar. But he was going to burn it all off sledding, and it was a special day.

"Of course," she told him, asking Melanie for both that and her own peppermint mocha as she ordered.

"Going to the sled races?" Melanie asked cheerfully, and Caroline nodded.

"Me and my friends are on one of the teams!" Jay piped up, and Melanie grinned.

"Good for you. Go get 'em, tiger," she said, pushing his hot chocolate across the counter to him and handing Caroline her coffee. "Have fun!"

They arrived at the sledding hill a short drive later, where Caroline saw other kids and their parents starting to assemble. Jay sprang out of the car before it had barely rolled to a stop, running to where

Caroline saw all of his friends gathered in a group—including Whitney, the girl from his class that he'd had a crush on last year. He hadn't said much more about it since then, but she could tell from the way he grinned at her and the pink on her cheeks as she smiled back that there was still very much a crush between those two.

Caroline smiled as she unbuckled Toby and put him in the baby sling that she strapped to her chest, her fleece-lined jacket nestled around them both. The excitement in the air was palpable, and she was even happier when she saw that her best friend, Audrey Felder, was standing in the small crowd as well. She walked over, waving as she did, and Audrey brightened as she saw Caroline.

"Hey, you!" She gave Caroline a one-sided hug, careful not to squish Toby. "I didn't think I'd see you cut loose from the inn today. I bet Jay is excited you're here."

"He is." Caroline let out a small, rueful chuckle. "Shelby was a good recommendation. She's running things so well that it wasn't even a big deal for me to take the day off and come out here."

Audrey gave her a knowing smile. She and Caroline had been friends since high school, and she knew Caroline as well as Caroline knew herself. She was practically another sister to her, and Caroline knew that she had already picked up on her reluctance to hand over the reins of running everything at the inn. "Having trouble letting go of things?"

Caroline smiled wryly. "You know me so well."

"Of course I do. I knew Shelby would be a good fit. I also knew she'd be patient with how neurotic you can be." Audrey smiled at her, a teasing glint in her eye. "You're very set in your ways, and since Shelby was a teacher, running her own track league, I knew she'd understand that."

"She has been very patient," Caroline admitted. "I can admit that I've been a lot to deal with. Picky and a bit critical."

"A bit?" Audrey raised a teasing eyebrow, and Caroline grimaced.

"Okay, probably a lot. But she *has* been patient. Which has gone a long way, I think. And she is very capable. I really *don't* have to worry about anything while she's there helping, I think, which should feel good, and it does. But also—"

"Like they'd be fine without you?" Audrey gave Caroline a knowing look, and Caroline sighed.

"Yeah."

"I get it. I don't run my own business, but my

kids are so close to both being grown up. Bennett is eighteen, he just came home on his first winter break from college. I want to call him every day, but I've had to stop myself, because I know it'll just smother him. And Kara is sixteen. She's got her *license*."

"Oh boy."

"Exactly!" Audrey shuddered. "I worry all the time. About her driving in the snow, driving at night, about whether or not she's being responsible. The list goes on. It's really hard to let go. Especially when it's someone whom you've gotten used to depending on you. And I think you get a little bit dependent on it too. Being needed feels good. But honestly, being wanted feels better." She smiled. "And I know when they call me or want to talk to me or spend time with me now, it's because they want to. I've accepted that it's different, but just as good."

"How did you get there?" Caroline asked, genuine sincerity in her voice. "I want to get to that place, I really do. I want to just be able to enjoy this new season where I have more time, and I can delegate, and spend more time with my family. But I keep feeling like something will go wrong. Like I'm selfish for wanting to be away from the inn, when it's been my parents' whole life, and then mine. Like if I love it, I shouldn't *want* to be away from it."

"Well, in terms of kids, I realized that if I forced it, if I smothered them, they'd start to resent me. They needed space, so they could breathe on their own, and then appreciate the time we get together. And honestly, the more room I've given them to figure out who they want to be at this age, the more they've come to me on their own."

"That's a good point."

Audrey nodded, smiling fondly. "Thanks. And I think in terms of the inn, if you don't take this opportunity, Caroline, *you* might come to resent *it*. Maybe you won't realize it at first, or maybe not for a long time, but you'll see eventually that you've missed out on time that you could have had because you couldn't let someone else take some of the work. Part of loving something and taking care of it is giving it space, I think. So that you do appreciate the effort that's put in when it is. Does that make sense?"

"Actually, it does," Caroline said thoughtfully. "It makes a lot of sense. And it's good advice for when my little ones get older too," she added.

"You should appreciate this time," Audrey said encouragingly. "In the blink of an eye, Jay and Toby will be as old as my kids! It'll go by so much faster than you realize. Embrace what Shelby is doing, and how much effort she's putting in to give you more time. And it's her job, after all! She's doing it well, and you should enjoy the space to have a little more of your own life."

Caroline nodded, taking a sip of her coffee as she watched the first teams starting to line up. She saw Bradley with the older kids, and Kara with a teenage boy she didn't recognize, talking animatedly. They were becoming young adults, and she felt a pang as she thought of Jay and Toby being that age.

Rhett and her mother and sisters had been right, she thought, and Audrey was right. It was hard to let go, but stifling herself and missing out because she was set in her ways wasn't good for anyone. It wouldn't become easy overnight, but she would learn to appreciate this new opportunity, and put her trust in Shelby that nothing terrible would happen because she'd taken some time for herself.

She was determined, at least, to try.

CHAPTER SEVENTEEN

Even feeling reassured that the wedding rings didn't make or break how much Spencer knew that she loved him and how excited she was about the wedding, Margo still hadn't been able to give up trying to find them. The result was that she was at her wit's end about it, because she still hadn't been able to figure out where they might have gone. She'd searched high and low, and she couldn't find them anywhere. She was running out of places to look, and no matter how many times she tried Nora's advice to try to retrack her steps, she just ended up feeling more confused, and like she was chasing her tail.

She'd finally decided to try the general store. Maybe, she thought as she drove over to Sugar Maple on her lunch break, she *hadn't* taken them with her.

Maybe she'd set them on the counter while they were taking all of the boxes and bags out to the car, and accidentally left them there, in her hurry to get Melanie dropped off at The Mellow Mug and get back to work.

It seemed unlikely, and she didn't know why Leon wouldn't have called her about it, but she couldn't think of anything else to try. She was running out of options, and time. And if they really were lost for good, she thought she should probably try to order replacements. At the very least, a stand-in for the wedding day until she *could* get them replaced. Necessary to prove their love or not, she couldn't quite imagine a wedding without an exchange of rings. It seemed like it would be a let-down, if not for her and Spencer, then for the guests.

She felt reluctant to tell Leon what had happened, even though she knew the kindly older man wouldn't judge her. But she still felt embarrassed for misplacing something so important. At this point, finding the rings was more important than her pride though.

"Hey there, Margo," Leon said with a grin. "Here for a deli sandwich? I can whip something up for you." He gestured to the counter in the back, where Margo knew the general store served a variety of hot, quick biscuit sandwiches in the morning and cold sandwiches in the afternoon. Everyone in Evergreen Hollow loved it, it was a quick alternative if you couldn't get out to Rockridge Grill to sit down or get takeout, especially during the lunch rush. The cold sandwiches made for a good, quick dinner too, sometimes.

"Normally, I would say yes," she said, her stomach growling at the thought of a cold-cut sandwich with all the fixings and a side of salt and vinegar chips. But she didn't have time for that today. "Actually though, I have something else going on." She chewed on her lower lip, feeling her face heat. "Remember how I sent out my wedding bands to have them engraved?"

Leon nodded. "I sure do. They came back pretty quick. Anything wrong with the order? Did they misspell something?"

Margo shook her head. "No—they were great when I looked at them. It's just..." She swallowed hard. "I can't find them anywhere," she admitted. "I thought I tucked them away in my room at home, but they're not there, and I've searched all over. My room, my office, my purse, camera bag, the car, everywhere I can think of that I might have stashed them without thinking or they might have dropped out. All of my coat pockets."

She frowned, chewing her lower lip. "I thought maybe I left them here and didn't realize it. Maybe I set them down on the counter and didn't actually grab them before leaving, even though I could have sworn I did."

"They weren't on the counter when I came back in from helping you girls," Leon said slowly. "I would've called you for sure if I'd seen them. But it's possible you tucked them in your pocket and they fell out in the back room, going back and forth and grabbing all of that stuff. Or..."

"Or what?"

He scratched his chin thoughtfully. "Bethany was helping out too. She might have swept them up, not realizing what it was, and tucked those little boxes away somewhere. She gets cleaning surges every now and again," he added with a grin. "But the trouble is, she doesn't really know where everything in the store goes. The grooming salon is her primary domain, and even though she helps out here, she's never quite figured out the method to my madness."

Margo clasped her hands together. "So maybe she accidentally moved them?"

He chuckled. "Possibly. We'll find those rings if

they're here. Come on, we'll look. You hop up on a ladder back there and check the storeroom shelves, and I'll look under the counter."

"Thank you!" Margo said eagerly, coming around the counter to head back to the stock room. "I haven't told Spencer I lost them," she added, pausing briefly. "I'm really hoping I never have to."

Leon patted her hand comfortingly. "We'll find those rings. He'll never need to be the wiser. Just a little mishap in the middle of all the wedding chaos, that's all."

Reassured, Margo headed back to the stock room. She found the ladder without any trouble, leaning it up against one of the well-organized shelves to start combing through them for the ring boxes, when she suddenly heard Spencer's voice from the front of the shop.

"Hey there, Leon. Thought I'd come and get a quick sandwich before I run back to the clinic. Maybe one for my head nurse, as well, she hasn't stopped all day. No time to run over to the Grill, but I'm starving—"

Margo jumped, nearly hitting her head and then almost slipping off of the ladder in her startlement. Her foot slid, and she grabbed the edge of a shelf, praying she wouldn't bring it all tumbling down. She clung to the ladder, swallowing hard as she tried to listen for what was going on out in the shopfront.

A stack of cookie tins rocked, and she grabbed them, gritting her teeth as they clanked together as she slid them further back onto the shelf. The ladder shifted as she did, and she stifled a yelp, hitting her elbow and nearly knocking over a set of wooden figurines that were neatly lined up next to her.

She gripped the ladder tightly, holding her breath as she tried not to fall or bring the whole storage room down around her, feeling clumsier than she ever had in her life. Or like a cartoon character, madly grabbing onto whatever she could to stay upright, all the while trying not to knock anything else over and somehow only managing to make more noise in the process.

She definitely didn't have a future as a cat burglar. Maybe the world's clumsiest cat.

"Did you hire someone to help out at the shop?" she heard Spencer ask jovially. "Sounds like they're taking the whole storeroom out back there. Or do you have mice?"

Oh no.

Margo swallowed hard, torn between climbing down the ladder and being afraid that if she did, she'd only knock into something else and cause another near-avalanche.

"Ah, must be Bethany back there," Leon said casually, and she heard him crossing the shop, probably headed over to the sandwich counter to draw Spencer away. "On one of her organizing kicks, I imagine."

"What am I doing?" Bethany's cheerful voice rang through the store as the little bell chimed that meant she'd emerged from the grooming salon on the other side, instantly exposing the white lie.

Margo squeezed her eyes tightly shut, her heart thumping. She'd been hoping so badly that she could just hide this entire disaster from Spencer, and that he'd never have to know that she'd almost lost their wedding rings. She knew he wouldn't be mad at her, and Nora believed that he wouldn't even be disappointed, but she wasn't a hundred percent sure about the latter. And she didn't think she could stand for him to be disappointed with her.

"Hey there, Spencer," Bethany said to him.

"Hi, Bethany!" Spencer greeted her in return, and Margo chewed on her lower lip. "Just grabbing a quick bite."

"I figured I'd get him in and out of here," Leon said cheerfully, but Margo could hear the hint of awkwardness as he tried to keep covering for her. She knew she should be using the time she had right that second to keep looking, but she was sure if she moved a muscle she'd cause some other racket, and then Spencer would have more questions. "Busy day for our town doctor."

"Well, you have a minute while Leon makes you your sandwich," Bethany said cheerfully, oblivious to the entire charade. "I was hoping you'd stop by sooner rather than later, I had something I wanted to show you."

"What's that?" Spencer asked, evidently distracted from the noise for the moment. Margo felt a brief burst of relief, but it was abruptly shattered when Bethany spoke again.

"Leon ordered a mystery shipment of Christmas ornaments, and a bunch of them were medical-themed! Cute nurse hats and stethoscopes and a little anatomically correct heart. Absolutely adorable. I thought they'd be perfect for your clinic Christmas tree." Two sets of footsteps came closer to the storage room, and Margo's breath caught as she realized Bethany was leading Spencer over to where she was.

"I'm actually just about done here. I think he's in a hurry, Bethany, " Leon called out, clearly trying to stop them, but from the sound of the footsteps getting closer, it seemed that he was failing.

"It'll just take a minute," Bethany insisted. "They really are so cute."

Margo's mind raced, knowing she only had seconds to come up with a plan. The best thing she could think of in the moment was saying that she'd started helping Leon out at the store, which made absolutely no sense, since she worked at *The Gazette* Monday through Friday. Also, Bethany would know that Leon had said nothing to her about any such thing, and she also didn't want to lie to Spencer. Which left her with very few options.

She looked around frantically, seeing a large stack of boxes at the back of the room. With no other plan that she could think of, she scrambled down the ladder and dashed into the dark corner, getting behind the boxes just as the door to the storage room opened and Bethany and Spencer walked in.

"Look," she heard Bethany saying. "There's this whole box."

There was the sound of Bethany dragging down a box and opening it.

"Leon, you need to put the ladder away!" Bethany yelled back out into the shop, and Margo heard Leon's answering grunt.

"These are the ones," Bethany said, and Margo crouched further behind the boxes, hoping that there wouldn't be that many ornaments, or maybe that Bethany wouldn't insist on showing Spencer each individual one.

"Those are cute," Spencer said agreeably. "I'm not sure if there's room on the clinic tree for any more ornaments, but I'll be sure to look. If there is, those would be perfect."

"I'll set them aside for you," Bethany said decisively.

"Oh, you don't have to—"

"Well, I can't imagine anyone else is going to be all that interested. They're perfect for your clinic." There was the sound of the box being closed and moved, and Margo bit her lip, hoping that she was almost home free.

"Spencer! Order up!" Leon called cheerfully from out in the back of the store.

"There's my cue," Spencer said. "I'll get back to you on that."

Just as Margo was almost certain that she'd gotten away with it, she felt her leg start to cramp. She shifted, desperate not for it to get bad enough that she'd make a sound, and her foot slid, her elbow going out to catch herself and knocking right into the stack of boxes next to her.

She gasped as the top half of the stack came tumbling down, leaving only the small amount of shadow that she was in to hide her.

Spencer looked around abruptly at the noise, just as he let Bethany walk out first, and his eyes widened with confused surprise as he saw Margo standing there uncertainly.

"Margo?" He frowned, looking entirely confused. "What are you doing back there?"

"I..." She swallowed hard, trying to think of an excuse. "Leon had some new decorations he thought we might like to use for the wedding. He wanted me to come in and look at them, so I decided to come in on my lunch break and have a look around. But he couldn't remember which boxes they were in, so I did some digging."

Spencer raised an eyebrow. "Did you find them?" He still looked confused, and Margo couldn't blame him. She knew she looked ridiculous, behind a stack of boxes in the back of the Sugar Maple storeroom.

"Um, yes! I think so." She reached down, grabbing the first thing she could find out of the box near her feet, and held it up.

Spencer's look of confusion only deepened, and Margo realized why a second later. She was holding up a neon orange feathered boa—the box was filled with them. They had absolutely no place in the wedding, and she honestly couldn't figure out why Leon had ordered them at all. Maybe for some sort of theme day at the school. It was the only possible explanation she could imagine, at least at the moment.

Spencer tilted his head, looking between the boa and Margo. "How does that fit with the wedding?" He walked closer to where she was standing, taking a look at the boa. "It's very—bright."

Margo could feel her face burning, and she felt sure that Spencer could see it too. "I—thought it would keep the guests' necks warm," she stammered, fully aware of how ridiculous every word sounded. "And it might add a pop of color. Everything is red and white, a little extra might... add something."

She trailed off, trying not to wince as she saw Spencer trying to make sense of what she was saying.

He smiled, leaning in to give her a kiss on the cheek.

"Maybe we should give that a little thought," he suggested. "You could even bring one home with you, see if you still like the color tomorrow. It's worth sleeping on."

Margo stifled a laugh, realizing that he thought the wedding stress was getting to her, and completely addling her senses. He had no idea just how accurate that really was.

"Okay," she agreed. "You should probably go get your sandwich."

"I should. I have to run back to the clinic. Have fun digging," he added, giving her another quick kiss and then hurrying out of the storeroom to grab his lunch order.

Margo chewed on her lower lip once he was gone, slumping against the wall as she tossed the boa back into the box. That had been a complete disaster, and she was still in the same predicament as ever.

She still couldn't find the rings.

CHAPTER EIGHTEEN

The fire crackled warmly as the credits started to roll on *How The Grinch Stole Christmas,* the Christmas movie that Caroline, Jay, and Rhett had all curled up in the living room to watch after she'd put Toby to bed. Jay and Rhett were still giggling over the jokes, Rhett mimicking the Grinch's voice, and Caroline smiled as she leaned back against the couch and watched them.

She'd left the inn at five today, on the dot, and she'd taken an hour's lunch break to come back to the house and eat with Jay and Toby. She hadn't stayed a minute later, and as a result, the house was spotless, they'd had a delicious dinner of winter squash casserole and garlic bread with fresh butter, and none of it had felt rushed.

She'd had the chores done by the time Rhett had gotten home from the fire station, which meant they'd been able to chat and catch up as she'd fixed dinner, and then they'd all sat around the table and talked. Jay had excitedly recounted the sled races to his father again, and Rhett had listened to every word as Caroline had fed Toby pureed squash in between bites of her own dinner.

And after, when Jay had asked if they could watch a Christmas movie once Toby was asleep, Caroline hadn't felt that she'd had to put anything off or feel guilty about leaving tasks undone to enjoy it. Everything had been taken care of, there were no issues at the inn, and she didn't have anything lingering around the house that she'd needed to do. The evening had been entirely hers, and as foreign as that felt, she'd really enjoyed it.

"Time for bed, mister," Rhett told Jay finally, getting up to stoke the fireplace. "Caroline, what about a glass of wine when I come back down?"

"That sounds perfect." She smiled at him, getting up as they did to go into the kitchen and pour a glass of wine for both herself and Rhett.

There was a pecan pie as well that Rhonda had made and sent home with her yesterday, and she cut a slice for each of them, finding the pretty Christmas-themed China dessert plates that she'd been gifted at her and Rhett's wedding and putting the pie on them. Rhonda firmly believed in the importance of holiday China, gifting a set to each of her daughters on their wedding days along with other important items, and she also strongly believed in *using* the good China, which she'd always imparted to her daughters as well.

She had it all set out when Rhett came back out, on the coffee table in front of the fire. He smiled as he sat down next to her on the couch, pulling her in close to them as they both balanced the plates on their laps.

"This has been a really nice evening," he said, leaning in to give her a light kiss. "You seem less stressed and tired than you have been in a long time."

"I feel less stressed and tired," Caroline admitted. "I guess I didn't realize just how much I'd run myself ragged until I started to slow down a little."

"I'm glad you hired Shelby," Rhett said, taking a bite of his pie. "I think having her at the inn has been good for you. I knew it would take some time to adjust, but I had faith it would be good in the end."

"It has taken some getting used to." Caroline reached for her wine glass, swirling it in the firelight.

"But it's freed me up a lot, and I'm definitely realizing that. It's not easy getting used to doing things differently, but the adjustment has definitely been worth it."

"I'm glad." Rhett smiled. "I'm happy to have you here more. And so is Jay."

"He hasn't stopped talking about how fun it was that I was there for the sledding tournament," Caroline said with a laugh. "I knew he would be happy, but it really meant a lot to him. Which made me realize how glad I was to be there. And when Toby started crawling yesterday, I was there for it, and I got to really slow down and enjoy every second. I got that video that I sent you, and I got to just soak in the moment. Before I had the extra help, I know I would have still enjoyed it, but I would have been thinking about a dozen other things too." She leaned into Rhett, resting her head against his shoulder for a moment. "I'm glad I listened and gave this a try. It really has made a difference."

"You're an amazing woman," Rhett said, tilting his head to look at her. "And accepting help doesn't change that a bit. It just means everyone who loves you gets to spend more time with you, so we can enjoy just how amazing you are."

Caroline smiled, laughing softly. "You're very sweet, you know that?"

"I try." He finished the last of the pie, setting down his plate. "And now that you have some extra time, I was even thinking we might go on a vacation sooner rather than later."

Caroline narrowed her eyes teasingly. "Don't push it, mister."

"I was thinking Jay's spring break." Rhett raised an eyebrow. "By then, you'll be even *more* used to having help. You'll practically be a lady of leisure. I was thinking we could go to New York, maybe. See the museums, check out a show, something like that."

"For how long?" Caroline chewed on her lip, feeling a small flutter of anxiety at the thought of leaving the inn to *that* degree. But she also felt a flicker of excitement. She hadn't ever really taken a vacation, and going on one with her family would be amazing. That sort of experience was exactly the reason why she had accepted the idea of hiring help at the inn in the first place.

"A few days. A long weekend. I can't get away from the fire station for all *that* long. But it would be a lot of fun," Rhett continued. "And I know Rhonda had a chat with you about this. She told me," he added.

Caroline knew exactly what he was talking about, because her mother *had* had a chat with her about exactly that, when she'd been chewing over the idea of hiring help. Rhonda had mentioned how she and Donovan had never gotten away for a trip together since their honeymoon, not until they'd gone on an anniversary trip back to Malibu last winter.

"She did say that she didn't regret how they did things, but that it would be good for me to not miss out on every opportunity to go on trips and adventures with my family because of the inn," Caroline admitted. "It was one of the reasons she was on board with hiring Shelby."

"Exactly." Rhett tightened his arm around her waist, holding her close. "I know the inn will always be important to you. You've put so much of yourself into it, and you've done an amazing job. But having some time to yourself, doing things together as a family, will only make you feel that much more rejuvenated when you come back."

"You're right," Caroline agreed. "And that time will be good for both of us. And for Jay, and Toby. Memories that all of us can make, together." She set her plate and glass down as well, curling in closer to Rhett next to the fire as she watched the flames leap and crackle. "I'm excited for our trip to New York."

She could tell Rhett was thrilled to hear her say that. He leaned in, dropping a kiss on top of her head as he squeezed her hand. "I can't wait to make plans with you."

"And with Margo's wedding so close," Caroline said thoughtfully, "this will give me more time to help with that. She misplaced something important for the wedding, and it's been stressing her out." She left it intentionally vague, not wanting to tell Rhett and then have him slip up and accidentally mention it to Spencer. She knew he'd never tell on purpose, but there was always the possibility of it slipping without him meaning for it to. "She can probably use all the help she can get hunting for it."

"See?" Rhett smiled, dropping another kiss on her hair. "Perfect timing."

Caroline hummed her agreement, luxuriating in the feeling of getting to simply sit and relax with her husband. The night had been wonderful, and she felt happier than ever, full of anticipation for the future.

More nights like this. Date nights out with Rhett. Her sister's wedding. Enjoying the holidays without being so overwhelmed from their busyness that she barely noticed all of the fun that there was to be had in her favorite season. And a vacation to look forward to, as well.

She let out a happy sigh, breathing in the scent of woodsmoke and pine, the warmth of her home wrapping around her and making her feel fully, truly relaxed.

This was, in fact, shaping up to be the best Christmas ever.

CHAPTER NINETEEN

It was almost completely dark as Margo tore through her car, pulling everything out and digging under all of the seats as she looked frantically for the rings.

She'd gotten off of work an hour ago, and she was running late for her date night with Spencer. She should have already gotten home and been getting ready—Spencer was supposed to be at the inn to meet her half an hour ago, and she was sure he must have texted her by now wondering where she was. But she was determined to find the rings. She knew she'd be distracted all night worrying about it, and she wanted to just be able to enjoy the evening with Spencer.

But now she'd created a whole other can of worms, by being late. She felt guilty, and she ran her hand through her hair, huffing out a frustrated breath as she looked at the mess she'd made. All of that, and she still hadn't found the rings. She had no earthly idea where they could be, and she had a feeling that she was just going to have to give up. She'd have to find a placeholder, and then re-order the specially engraved rings. The wedding was only a week away, there wasn't time to get the engraved rings all over again.

Feeling defeated, she threw away the trash she'd cleaned out of her car and rearranged everything else, sliding into the driver's seat and starting it up. She needed to get to the inn and meet Spencer for their date, before he really started to worry.

Of course, Spencer was waiting in the living room of the inn when she walked inside. She hurried over, giving him an apologetic kiss. "I'm so sorry I'm late," she said in a rush. "I got held up, and—"

"Don't worry about it," Spencer reassured her, returning the kiss. "I'm sure you want to change out of your work clothes. I'll just wait here, there's no rush."

"I can go like this," Margo protested, but Spencer shook his head, chuckling.

"I know you want to change before we go. It's

really fine, Margo. I promise. I'm perfectly comfortable here waiting, and I have been."

"I shouldn't have been late." She twisted her lips, still feeling apologetic. "That wasn't respectful of your time at all, when I know you've been so busy lately. You probably would have rather spent that half hour at *your* home relaxing, instead of waiting around in mine."

Spencer took her hand, stopping her short. "A place isn't my home, Margo," he said sincerely. "You are." He tugged her forward, close to him, leaning in to whisper in her ear. "My heart has found its home."

She jerked backward, stunned, as her eyes widened. There was only one reason for him to say that.

But how...?

Spencer slipped a hand into the pocket of his chinos, producing the two small blue velvet boxes that she'd been searching for endlessly. He was smiling at her, amused and adoring all at the same time, and Margo's mouth dropped open.

"Where did you *find* those?" she asked, gasping, and Spencer laughed.

"In the spice cabinet, for some reason? I was getting nutmeg for some tea, and they were right there. I thought maybe you had hidden them there on purpose, forgetting how much I love to top *everything* I drink with something from your mother's extensive spice cabinet, but Rhonda came in and saw them and told me you'd been looking for them all over." He chuckled, setting them down on the coffee table. "I don't suppose looking for them had something to do with why you were hiding in Leon's storeroom, making up ridiculous stories about orange boas?"

"Oh!" Margo covered her face with her hands, thoroughly embarrassed. "I can't believe this."

"So it definitely wasn't on purpose, then." Spencer still sounded amused. "Care to tell me how our wedding rings ended up in your mother's spice cabinet? It sounds like a good story."

Margo was sure she was going to sink into the floor, her face on fire.

"I remember now," she mumbled, rubbing her hands over her face as the pieces she'd been trying to figure out for days finally clicked into place. "I had them with me when I came home from work. And I stopped in the kitchen before I went upstairs, to make myself an eggnog steamer for a treat after work. Mom came in, so of course I showed her the rings while I was working on it. I set them on the counter, and I was so frazzled that day with all of the decorations coming in, and work, and planning. I must have swept them up with the cinnamon after putting it on my drink, and put them in the cabinet by mistake."

"That's an amazing story," Spencer said with a laugh. "I can't wait to tell that one at every Christmas from now on."

"*Stop.*" Margo's eyes widened, but his laughter was infectious, and she felt herself starting to giggle too. "I can't believe I did that."

"I absolutely can," Spencer said. "And I love you for it."

"I've been looking *everywhere* for them," she said plaintively. "My room, my car, my purse, my office—"

"Leon's store?" Spencer supplied, looking as if he were about to break into fresh laughter. "I know. I was there."

Margo started to laugh too, but stopped abruptly as the rest of what Spencer finding the rings meant, hit her. "The rings aren't a surprise now," she said sadly. "I had this whole plan for you to see them at the wedding for the first time, and now you know all about it."

Spencer sobered instantly, the laughter fleeing as he saw the distress on her face.

"That doesn't take away from the significance of the gesture at all, Margo," he said gently, still holding her hands in his. "In fact, if anything, it makes me that much more eager to wear it, knowing you thought to engrave something so special inside of the ring for me. For *us*.'"

Margo nodded, biting her lip. "I know things were rocky sometimes, with me staying here in Evergreen Hollow," she said softly. "I never intended to stay, initially. I thought I would just be here for a couple of months and then move on. And then when I broke my leg, I still didn't plan on putting down roots. But even though I knew I was going to move on, I wanted to be with you every time I saw you. You made me laugh, and made me happy, and I was so glad to see you every time you came around."

She smiled shyly at him, and Spencer squeezed her hands gently again.

"I felt the same way," he told her quietly. "I knew I would have to let you go if you wanted to leave, but I couldn't resist being around you. You were like a light, like a firefly in summer, and I loved watching you. I loved seeing you. I loved hearing your laugh. I wanted to be with you even if it was only for a little while. And when you decided to stay, it was the happiest moment of my life."

"I know you worried about me being able to put down roots and be happy though," Margo said, remembering the last Christmas, and how Spencer had feared she was getting restless. "I wanted to show you that I don't have any doubts any longer, and I don't feel restless or fidgety. I don't know if I'll ever be as good of a cook as my mother, or if I won't lose my keys, or if I'll remember all of the groceries even when I have a list, but I do know I want to stay here with you forever. I'm happy here, and I never want to be anywhere else but home. With you—*my* home," she added, her eyes bright as she looked at him earnestly. "You are my home too, Spencer."

"And you always will be mine, as well." He leaned in, kissing her there in front of the fire, the romantic words hovering in the air between them. "And I hope that you remember all of that to write it down," he added with a teasing smile as he pulled back. "Because if you haven't already written your wedding vows, those were perfect."

Margo felt herself smile so widely that she thought her face might crack. "I can't wait to say them again," she whispered, as she leaned in for another kiss. "I can't wait to become your wife."

CHAPTER TWENTY

The day of Margo and Spencer's wedding, Caroline was in full big-sister mode, determined to make certain that everything went off without a hitch. As a part of the bridal party, she'd already gotten ready, but she had on her boots underneath her cranberry-red dress, her heels in the car waiting. After all, the food for the reception still needed to be loaded up, and she wasn't about to carry things back and forth in high heels.

Her wedding gift to Margo, besides helping Rhonda prepare all of the food, was wearing a pair of heels at all. The last time she'd put them on had been for her own wedding.

She had to admit, if she was going to get dressed up though, this was a wonderful occasion for it. And it had been worth it to see Rhett's face when she'd come out of the bathroom earlier, in the cranberry silk dress that Margo had picked out for her bridesmaids, with the long lace sleeves and sweetheart neckline. She'd done her hair, curling it and putting it up in a fancy updo, and found the pearl earrings that she'd worn for her own wedding. Rhett's jaw had almost hit the floor when she'd walked out.

He had looked incredibly handsome in his charcoal suit as well, with the holly boutonniere that all of Spencer's groomsmen would be wearing. Jay was equally spiffy in his own matching suit, and they'd even gotten the tiniest of baby suits for Toby to wear.

The whole family, in fact, looked amazing in all of their best clothes, and the dresses that Margo had picked out. Nora was wearing a matching cranberry dress, and Madison had a small red and gold dress that made her look like a little Christmas gift all wrapped up. Aiden was also one of the groomsmen, wearing a charcoal suit, and Rhonda had gotten a beautiful deep green mother-of-the-bride dress, made of a beautiful shimmering taffeta that caught the light every time she moved. She was wearing her own set of pearls, from her wedding day, another of the Stoker traditions. Every bride got her own set of pearls, and Caroline knew her mother would be gifting Margo with hers when she was finished getting ready.

Caroline hurried back into the inn, where she found Shelby in the kitchen, carefully packaging up the cut vegetables for the salad first course. She and Rhonda had planned on preparing the food for the reception since the earliest stages of planning Margo's wedding, but Shelby had overheard them discussing it and eagerly offered her help. Now, dressed in a pretty winter blue dress and heels, she covered the last of the containers and set them in a neat line to be taken out to the waiting car.

"How is everything going?" Caroline asked, and Shelby looked back at the counter, surveying her work.

"Everything is right on schedule," she said confidently. "I already sent the rest of the cold foods out with your dad. It's all being transported to the reception venue. This is the last of it."

Caroline smiled, and it struck her in that moment how much more she was getting to enjoy this day, as with so many other things lately, because she had an extra pair of hands that were so willing to help.

"You've been so helpful, Shelby," she said sincerely. "This is outside the scope of your actual job, but you volunteered. And Mom and I, and Margo and Nora, appreciate it so much. I'm so thankful we have you today, and that your help has given me so much extra time lately. I've gotten to spend more time with Rhett, and my children, and it really has been the best Christmas gift anyone could have possibly given me."

Shelby beamed, a broad smile spreading across her face. "That's all I want," she said sincerely. "To be helpful, without overstepping. I love working here, and I'm so happy that I'm getting to be a part of this special day. I love weddings," she added. "Especially Christmas weddings. They're the best."

"You're doing an amazing job," Caroline assured her. "And I'm so glad that you're here too, and that we got to know you in time for you to celebrate Margo's wedding with the family. This is very special for all of us."

"I know you didn't want to let someone who wasn't family have a hand in the inn at first," Shelby said with a smile, her expression letting Caroline know that she completely understood. "But I feel like I'm a little closer to that, after today."

"You absolutely are." Caroline glanced at her

phone, and then at the stack of containers still on the counter. "Can you get these out to the car? I want to go see how Margo is doing."

"Absolutely," Shelby said, reaching for the first of the stack and heading out to where Caroline's Subaru was parked.

Caroline hurried up the stairs to the upper floor, where Margo was getting ready in her bedroom. Nora and Rhonda were both inside, Madison babbling away happily in Nora's arms, and Caroline gasped as Margo turned around and she saw her sister in her full bridal attire for the first time.

Margo looked absolutely stunning. The simple white dress, made of soft lace all over with an eyelash fringe at the wrists and hem, hugged Margo in a perfect, wintry column. The high, square neckline was beautiful, showcasing the strand of pearls at Margo's neck and the pearl drop earrings she was wearing, and the white fur stole around her shoulders was the perfect winter touch to the gown. Her hair was loose, in large, thick princess curls, and Rhonda was sliding the veil edged in the same eyelash lace into her hair just as Caroline walked in.

"You look like a bride!" Caroline exclaimed, feeling her eyes mist over with happy tears at seeing her youngest sister all dressed up for her wedding.

"I do, don't I?" Margo was beaming as she turned to look in the mirror again, taking in her appearance. "I love the pearls that Mom gave me."

"I try to make sure each of you has a set that suits you," Rhonda said, looking at her three daughters with a soft expression on her face.

"You did a perfect job, picking them out," Caroline said, and she meant it. Her own pearls, that she was wearing again today, were a simple single strand at her neck and a pair of plain, round studs for her earrings. Simple and minimalist. Nora's was a strand interspersed with a small diamond between each pearl, with drop earrings that threaded through her ears and had another small diamond tipped at the end of each pearl—a little more stylish and flashy, like her taste had tended toward before she'd moved home, and sometimes still did.

And Margo's were perfect for her too. She also had a single strand, and earrings that dropped down from a thin white-gold stud at her ears, but they were black pearls, with the same purple-green shimmer as the tanzanite ring on her finger. Simple, classic, but unique—and perfectly suited to her.

"I'm so happy," Margo said, that smile still lighting up her face. "I'm so glad you all talked me into having the whole big wedding. Now that it's here, I can't wait for all of it. To marry Spencer, and celebrate with all of you."

Rhonda checked the veil once more to make sure it would stay in Margo's hair, secured with a white-gold hair comb that had small sapphires in it for Margo's 'something blue'. Her pearls were her 'something new', as her sisters' had been, and her 'something old' was a filigreed silver ring Rhonda had had for years, that Donovan had given her when they'd first started dating. It served as her 'something borrowed' too, since Rhonda had teasingly told her that she absolutely wanted it back after the wedding.

"I'm so glad you're here with me too," Margo said, looking at Caroline and Nora. "I missed your weddings, but you're here at mine, and that means so much."

"We wouldn't miss it for the world," Caroline assured her, and Nora echoed it. "Not a chance. Now, we should probably get downstairs. We can't have you running late to your own wedding."

Margo beamed, as her mother and sisters came in to hug her, each of them gently embracing her so as not to crush her dress and veil. By the time they all disentangled themselves, everyone was misting over with happy tears, and Nora grabbed a box of tissues, passing it around as all four women tried to dab at their eyes without ruining their makeup.

"I'll help you with your veil," Caroline said, picking up the end of it as Margo prepared to head downstairs. "Let's get you married."

Donovan was waiting outside, with what Margo had said was her favorite part of all of the wedding planning. They'd borrowed a sleigh and horses to take her to the church, the same sleigh that Spencer had borrowed two years ago, to take her on her first date to see the holiday fireworks. She'd wanted to go so badly, despite her broken leg and the impossibility of the hike, and Spencer had found a thoroughly romantic way to make her dreams come true.

Margo climbed into the sleigh, as Caroline helped fold her skirt and veil into it, tucking the fur-lined blanket around her. "We'll meet you there!" she said, heading with Nora to the car that they would all pile into, as Rhonda got into the sleigh next to Margo to ride with her.

Nora turned on the Christmas station as she and Caroline climbed into the car, Madison buckled into the car seat in the back. Rhett would already be at the church by now with Aiden, watching Jay and Toby until Shelby got there and could take over with Toby. Jay was the ringbearer, so he had a very important part to play. He'd found out a few days ago about Margo's mishaps with the ring, and had teased her mercilessly about it, promising to make sure to bring cinnamon to the ceremony.

It was one of those stories, Caroline knew, that would be told forever around the holidays, reminding them of all these happy moments that they were sharing together, at a time of year that all of them had reason to love.

They followed the sleigh to the church, a slow procession. All the stores on Main Street were closed, with everyone invited to the wedding. In such a small town, a wedding was practically a holiday in and of itself, and everyone was gathering at the church to see Margo and Spencer get married. Caroline and Nora's weddings had been the same, and while she'd been a bit overwhelmed by it all at the time, now Caroline looked back on it fondly, excited for Margo to have the same, wonderful day.

As they pulled up in front of the church, she saw the sleigh come to a stop, Donovan getting out to come around and help his wife and daughter out onto the steps. And Caroline felt a warm glow, filling her with happiness as she slipped out of the car with Nora, ready for a wedding.

All of her family was here, at home, for good.

And she was able to truly relax and enjoy it, in a way that she never had been able to before.

* * *

As Margo stepped out of the sleigh, butterflies filled her stomach, fluttering through her as she realized that in just a few short minutes, she would be walking down the aisle.

The entire day had been perfect. Rhonda had brought her breakfast in bed that morning, as she had for all of her daughters on their wedding day, making Margo's favorite breakfast of bacon, maple brioche French toast, and pumpkin spice coffee, along with a mimosa and a bowl of fresh fruit. She'd sat with Margo as Margo had done her best to eat despite her excited nerves, reminiscing about her own wedding day and answering all of Margo's nervous questions as they'd waited for Nora and Caroline to arrive.

Margo had wanted to know how her parents had stayed in love for so long, and Rhonda told her that it was the same answer she'd given Nora, which Nora had told Margo not all that long ago, in Margo's office as they'd been searching for the rings.

"There will be plenty of difficult times," Rhonda had told her. "But through it all, as long as you face them together, as a team, all of those times will make you stronger, and make the good moments so much better. And all of the good moments, all of the memories small and large, accumulate to make a life together. That's all there is to it. It's you and Spencer, and the life you want to build together, the two of you."

They'd sat and talked, just the two of them, until Nora had arrived with Madison to help Margo do her hair and makeup. Caroline had poked her head in shortly after, checking in on them and bringing up a fresh round of mimosas before she'd headed back down to help with the food. And as Margo had watched herself transform into a bride, she felt like she was in a fairytale—in a dream, really.

But it was all real, and in a moment, she would see Spencer, and they would start their happily ever after.

Donovan tucked his arm through hers, as the music started inside of the church and Margo felt those butterflies take flight again. Everyone else was lined up—Jay with the rings on a blue velvet pillow, Caroline just behind him, and Nora behind her, with Margo bringing up the rear. Even Chessie had been given a part in the festivities, and as the doors opened Nora set her down, letting her run down the aisle to where Aiden stood with a treat in his hand. A small silk bag had been attached to her leash, a slit in it so that as it dragged behind her it would spill flower petals all over the aisle. Margo pressed a hand to her mouth through her veil, stifling a giggle as she watched Chessie spring down the aisle, scattering petals everywhere as she ran to Aiden, who picked her up and passed her over to Shelby.

And then, it was time to head down the aisle. Margo's heart, which had been racing nonstop, settled in an instant as soon as she saw her groom. Spencer stood at the end of the aisle in his perfectly tailored charcoal suit, his eyes widening as he saw her, and she felt sure that she saw them mist over as she drew closer.

Donovan led her up to the aisle, placing her hand in Spencer's, and she felt all of those butterflies take flight again.

When it came time for their vows, she remembered what she had said to him in the living room when he'd found their rings, and she repeated it word for word, right down to the bit about the grocery list. Spencer's smile grew with every word, his whole face alight with adoration, and when it came time for his vows, he finished with a sentence that made her heart flip in her chest.

"My heart has found its home."

She felt her eyes fill with happy tears as he slipped the wedding band on her finger and she did the same for him, knowing that those few words, that meant so much to them, were close to their hearts forever now. And when he pulled her in for a kiss, all of the guests erupting in applause, she didn't know if it was possible to be any happier than she was in that moment.

"Wait until you see the surprise I have outside," she whispered as they headed down the aisle, hand in hand, man and wife, as the guests threw rose petals all around them.

"Another surprise?" Spencer asked curiously, and then she saw his eyes widen when they stepped outside into the cold, and he saw the sleigh.

"Our first date." Margo beamed at him. "I thought it was romantic."

"It's the most romantic thing you could have come up with," he assured her, and he pulled her into his arms, kissing her again right there in front of the sleigh, as the guests spilled out around them.

Tucked into the furs in the sleigh, as the horses pulled away from the church toward the event center where the reception would be held, Spencer slipped his hand into hers. And he held it the whole way there, as the snow flurried around them and the Christmas lights twinkled all along Main Street, until the sleigh stopped in front of the venue and Spencer climbed out of the sleigh to help Margo out.

Rhonda and Caroline had planned the menu, and it was all of Spencer and Margo's favorite foods.

The first course was an appetizer of baked New England clams, Spencer's favorite, and Margo's favorite winter salad that Rhonda always made. The salad included winter greens with goat cheese, dried cranberries, orange slices, and a vinaigrette to finish it off. It was followed by a delicious butternut squash bisque, a favorite of both the bride and groom, and then the choice of entrees.

There was Spencer's favorite, red-wine braised venison brisket with a side of roasted vegetables and garlic mashed potatoes, Margo's favorite orange-basted duck breast with the same, or an option of locally caught fish, dressed with herbs and lemon and served with a side of lobster risotto and Rhonda's famous baked squash. And, of course, there would be wedding cake for dessert, but also the bride and groom's favorite desserts—creme brûlée and fudge, respectively.

Margo and Spencer hadn't known what to pick out of all of the delicious options, and they were thrilled to find that plates had been arranged for them that had a little of each. They sat next to each other at the sweetheart table, feeding each other bites of dinner, and Margo heard the click of the disposable cameras as the guests were already taking pictures of the festivities.

The wedding cake, when it was brought out, was perfect. Margo had wanted a simple cake, with white frosting and winter flowers as the decoration, in her and Spencer's favorite flavor of carrot cake with cream cheese filling.

He gingerly fed her a piece, careful of her makeup, and she did the same for him, as she heard more of the clicking of guests taking pictures. The sound filled her with happiness, and she was beyond glad that she'd chosen that option for their wedding photos. They might not be professional photos, but she couldn't wait to see all of the moments that the people they loved most had thought were important enough to capture forever.

The first dance was everything that she could have hoped for too. She felt happy tears well up in her eyes again at the first notes of *I'll Be Home For Christmas*, and she sighed as Spencer wrapped his arms around her, swaying with her on the dance floor for the first few lines of the song before the other couples began to join them.

They had planned this together, and as the song went on, Nora and Aiden, Caroline and Rhett, and Rhonda and Donovan all joined them out on the dance floor, swaying to the music as it filled the room.

The four couples danced, glancing joyfully at each other as they spun around the floor, and Margo felt her eyes mist over with an overwhelming emotion of happiness.

"Every Christmas since I've been home has been wonderful," she whispered in Spencer's ear as the music began to fade out and he pulled her in close. "But I think this is my favorite of them all so far."

He smiled, pressing a kiss next to her ear. "We'll just have to figure out how to top it next year, then."

The music picked up again, a festive array of Christmas music from a variety of countries and traditions, a nod to Margo's jet-setting days, interspersed with familiar favorites. The reception space was filled with guests mingling, going to the bar for the two drinks specially crafted for the day—apple cider and whiskey with a cinnamon stick for the groom's drink, and a cranberry apple spritzer for the bride's—or going to the non-alcoholic bar that offered a variety of hot cocoas and hot apple ciders. There was peppermint, caramel, and spiced options for the hot cocoa, as well as mulled, pumpkin, and cherry apple ciders, served hot.

Partway through, there was a brief lull once again as everyone gathered around for toasts and speeches. Donovan went up first, smiling broadly at Margo and Spencer as he began to speak.

"As everyone knows," he began, "last year had a bit of a scare for me and my family. I'm so grateful to be here this Christmas, to see my youngest daughter get married, and welcome my new son into the family. I've already been given two wonderful sons from Nora and Caroline's marriages, and Aiden and Rhett are as loved by me and Rhonda as if they were our own. My family has always been the most important part of my life, and I'm so glad to have seen it expand in such a way, not only from my daughters' marriages, but the grandchildren I have now as well. Margo and Spencer, I know there are years of joy and wedded bliss ahead of you, and I'm looking forward to every day that I get to witness that as your father."

He smiled, lifting his glass, and the rest of the room toasted to his speech. Margo's eyes were misty, and she saw her mother delicately wiping underneath hers, clearly on the verge of crying her own happy tears.

Spencer squeezed her hand, and then got up, making his way to the small stage.

"I didn't expect to have to follow that," he said with a laugh, looking over at the gathered guests. "But my sentiments are very much the same. I've never been given a more wonderful or life-changing Christmas gift than I was the winter that Margo Stoker arrived in my life, and I've been endlessly grateful every day since that she decided to stay and make Evergreen Hollow her home once again. I've been given not only her love and the promise of having it forever, but the added gift of her wonderful and loving family, who has surrounded me and filled spaces in my heart that were in need of that kind of love. And I will forever be glad to have Rhonda, and Donovan, Nora and Aiden, Caroline and Rhett as a part of my family now as well."

He smiled, his gaze locking with Margo's as a mischievous expression crossed his face. "And, on a much lighter note, I have a special surprise for my new bride."

Margo looked at him quizzically, utterly confused, and then pressed her hands over her mouth to stifle peals of laughter as Spencer drew a long, neon orange feathered boa out of his suit jacket. "Despite my objections, I know my wife was dead-set on having this little touch at the wedding. 'Some added color' I think her words were. So please, enjoy. She thought you might need the extra warmth too, to ward off the chill." He grinned as Margo covered her face with her hands, her shoulders shaking with laughter as the ushers passed out boas to all the guests. Her new husband was still smirking at her when she looked up, as he made his way back down to her, and when she looked over at Leon she saw him chuckling as well.

She rose up from her seat as Spencer came over to her, pressing her hands to his face as she drew him in for a kiss. She heard the guests clapping as he wrapped his arm around her waist, prolonging the kiss for a moment longer, and then she touched her forehead to his as she smiled up at him.

"I can't wait to start our life together," she said softly. "And I've never been more happy—or felt more at home."

CHAPTER TWENTY-ONE

The Monday before Christmas, Nora had taken Madison and gone to visit a couple of her cousins in Burlington, wanting to see a Christmas light show. It had been a fun day, out on her own, getting a bit of a breather now that the flurry of wedding planning was finished. There was plenty of holiday planning left to do—gifts to wrap and parties to go to, her own annual Christmas party to host, and shopping to finish. But she could get a good bit of that shopping done in Burlington, and she'd bundled Madison up, grabbed her list, and headed out for a refreshing day out of town.

Caroline had agreed to watch Chessie for the day, letting the puppy tear around her own small cottage. Jay had been thoroughly enthused by the idea, excited to run around in the snow with Chessie, and Toby had seemed as immediately taken by the small dog as Madison was. Nora had high hopes that by the time she got home, Chessie would be thoroughly worn out from playing with Jay all afternoon.

Her own day had been absolutely lovely. She'd gotten a peppermint mocha to go from The Mellow Mug before heading out, chatting with Melanie for a few minutes about holiday plans and Christmas parties, and sharing their excitement over the holiday. Nora was particularly excited for this Christmas, now that Madison was a little bit older, and could enjoy the holiday more. She was still very small, but Nora could see her getting excited about the lights and music and smells of Christmas, pictures with Santa and the sleigh that came through Main Street occasionally this close to the holiday for the children, with reindeer antlers on the horses' bridles.

Driving to Burlington on the crisp, sunny winter day with Christmas music playing and the whole afternoon ahead of her had been wonderful, as well. She'd crossed off almost all of her Christmas list—a new pair of well-made leather work gloves for her father, a new hardback release that Rhonda had been excited to read, a travel journal for Margo to take on her honeymoon and a gift card to L.L. Bean for Caroline. That last one had become a bit of a tradition between the sisters—Caroline avoided shopping whenever possible and Nora loved it, so since she'd come home, they'd made an annual excursion of going shopping to refresh Caroline's wardrobe after Christmas, using the gift card that Nora always got her. Otherwise, Caroline would always come up with something that money needed to be used for more, and would never actually go.

She'd picked up a video game for Jay and new toys for Toby, as well as an adorable little snowsuit that she couldn't resist. She'd gotten Rhett a subscription for monthly flavored coffee beans, knowing Caroline had gotten him a new, fancy coffeemaker that he'd wanted, and for Spencer, she'd gotten an array of hot and barbecue sauces from a local place in Burlington, since he'd been trying to cook more for himself and Margo. For Aiden, she'd found a new watch, carved out of maple from a local jeweler, and she knew he'd love it. He'd only ever wear it out for special occasions, she knew, but it was a nod to his lifetime love of carpentry, and a special gift. She'd even had it engraved, inspired by Margo engraving her and Spencer's wedding rings.

It was the last thing she picked up before heading to the light show, and her heart flipped a little when she saw the engraving carved underneath the face.

I found you at exactly the right time. Their wedding date was underneath it, and she smiled, thinking of the look on his face when he unwrapped it at Christmas.

She'd had a lovely lunch, just her and Madison, at a little Irish pub that she'd been to before with her mother and sisters. There had been a table open by the fireplace, and she'd gotten a lamb wrap with Dijon maple sauce and a glass of cider, people-watching as she luxuriously enjoyed her lunch with plenty of time to spare.

Her cousins had met her at the light show, which was a huge event, complete with live Christmas music and food trucks, as well as stations serving hot apple cider, mulled wine, and hot cocoa. They'd reminisced over how wonderful Margo's wedding had been, and Nora had enjoyed getting to describe all the little details she'd labored over for so long planning it. There were bigger weddings, bigger events that she'd planned when she lived in Boston, but none of them had ever felt as special to her.

After the light show, they all hugged farewell,

and she headed back home to Evergreen Hollow, packages all piled up in the backseat. She'd enjoyed the day out, but she was eager to get home and see Aiden. And she was also a tiny bit concerned that Chessie would be driving him mad. Caroline would have dropped her back off at the house by now, and while Nora was hopeful that the puppy would have gotten her energy out, she also knew that it was sometimes seemingly boundless.

She walked in, setting her bags down as she knocked the snow off of her boots and shed her coat and gloves. The house was quiet other than the low hum of the television turned on as background noise, and as she carefully stepped into the living room, she saw that it was empty.

Aiden must have gone up to bed, she thought, switching off the television and dampening the fire, storing her shopping bags in the linen closet until tomorrow when she would go through and wrap them all. There were no sounds of barking or other life, the kitchen entirely clean, and she smiled fondly as she realized that Aiden had spent some of his evening cleaning up for her. He would have come in late, finishing up the last of his projects before he took a break for the holidays, and she imagined he'd probably brought home takeout for himself from the

Grill. But still, there were obvious signs that he'd cleaned the kitchen and tidied the living room for her, and she felt a wave of affection at the thought.

Carefully, she carried Madison upstairs, staying as quiet as she could as she put her daughter down to sleep. She turned on the monitor and nightlight, waiting for a few minutes until Madison's breathing was soft and even before slipping back out into the hall, heading to the master bedroom.

As soon as she stepped inside, she saw Aiden. He was sleeping peacefully atop the covers, Chessie curled up with one paw over her nose on the pillow, buried in the crook of his neck.

It was an utterly adorable sight. Nora stood there for a few moments, taking it in, enchanted by the picture of her handsome husband and the adorable puppy cuddled up there together, snoozing away. She couldn't quite pull herself away, not until Chessie heard her shift against the doorframe and opened her eyes, tail immediately wagging enthusiastically as she saw Nora.

The puppy twisted around before Nora could head to get her, licking Aiden's cheek as if to wake him up and say *look, Nora's home!* He groaned at first, but Chessie didn't stop, and his eyes flickered open a moment later.

"Stop that, you," he grumbled teasingly, grabbing the puppy and putting her in the crook of his arm as he rolled over. He saw Nora then, walking toward the bed, and a broad smile creased his handsome face.

"You know," Nora said with a small smirk, "Bethany talked us into fostering Chessie—and into continuing to foster her when she was being such a pain—because she convinced me it would be good for Madison. But I think she's good for *you*." She couldn't help but smile, seeing Chessie tuck herself closer to Aiden's broad chest. "Looks like you need her as much as Madison does."

"She's charming," Aiden admitted, ducking his head to avoid another lashing from Chessie's tongue. The puppy squirmed out of his grip, bounding across the mattress toward Nora as she headed to the dresser to change for bed. "But we've all gotten attached to her, I think." A smile played across his lips. "We should just adopt her already. Tell Bethany that we're keeping her. I think she assumes as much —she still has the pictures up at the groomer's, but I think she's all but given up on finding Chessie a different home. One time I stopped by the general store and mentioned it, she said she thought Chessie had already found one."

"She said the same thing to me," Nora admitted. "But Aiden, she's disrupted our schedule so much. We had everything down perfectly with Madison after last Christmas, and things were so peaceful all year. We really got into a rhythm. Now it's all been upended, and I'm falling behind, chasing both of them around all day. What about when I start adding more to my planning calendar after the new year? Now that Margo's wedding is finished, I planned on taking a couple more clients from here, or nearby. I met one woman tonight at the light show in Burlington who was interested in having me plan a graduation party for her son."

"That's fantastic!" Aiden smiled at her encouragingly. "We said there'd be more time for you to get back to work next year, with Madison being a little older. It sounds like that's all falling right into place."

"Right—but it's all hectic now because of Chessie. She's not as crazy as a second baby, but she's a little tornado. She gets into more trouble than Madison sometimes, and she can certainly be just as loud," Nora pointed out.

"It's just a learning curve," Aiden said confidently. "There was one with Madison, finding a rhythm with her, and like you said, we did it. We got into a groove, and everything was fine. We can do the same thing adding a puppy to the mix. Besides," he added with a grin. "It's good practice. For Madison, sharing her time and our attention, and for us—you know, in case we decide to have another baby."

Nora rolled her eyes playfully. "Bethany said the same thing in regards to that too."

"She's very smart." Aiden nodded sagely. "We should take her advice."

He broke off, turning to look curiously under his pillow. "What is that—why is there a sock under my pillow?"

Nora started laughing. "It's from Chessie, I'm sure," she said between giggles. "She upended that laundry basket and took it all over the house before I caught her. I'm going to be finding what that little rascal scattered through the house all the way until next Christmas."

Aiden chuckled. "It'll be like shopping. Finding items we forgot we had all year long."

Nora was still laughing as she sank down onto the edge of the bed, Chessie immediately clambering into her lap. "Okay," she said after a moment, scratching behind the puppy's ears as she looked over at Aiden. "I give in."

Aiden grinned, reaching for her to pull her back

against the mound of pillows with him, Chessie still in her lap. "Does that mean...?"

"Yes." She leaned over to kiss him, Chessie jumping up to lick her face at the same moment. "We can keep the puppy."

CHAPTER TWENTY-TWO

Margo looked around her new surroundings, feeling a burst of happiness.

She was finally all moved into Spencer's—now *their*—house, and she had loved every second of getting situated. It was just in time too. Christmas was tomorrow, and she was so excited to get ready to go over to the inn together with Spencer, and come home with him in the evening.

It would be their first Christmas getting to do that, instead of her kissing him goodnight at the end of the evening and then staying to wind down in front of the fire before going upstairs to her bedroom at the inn, and the novelty of it had her giddy with excitement.

She knew Spencer was looking forward to their

first Christmas together as a married couple too. He was working late, finishing up a final few things at the clinic so that they could enjoy the holidays without distraction—barring any unforeseen accidents that might pull him away, a doctor's work was never truly done—and she was curled up on the couch in front of the fireplace.

The living room had a bit of her touch now, as did everything else. The kitchen was now full of wedding gifts: a new China set from her parents, shiny new wine glasses, a Dutch oven, a fancy espresso machine. Their bedroom had her desk tucked into a corner now, the bedding changed out for a pretty floral bedspread that she and Spencer had picked out together, made up with dark green sheets as a nod to the season.

She'd brought her throw pillows and favorite quilt to put on the sectional couch in Spencer's living room, and favorite photos that she'd taken over the years were framed on the walls. It was truly beginning to feel like *their* space, in every sense of the word, and she was so glad that Spencer hadn't minded all the changes to his family home. If anything, he'd encouraged her, excited to see what she would do to liven up the space.

Now, she opened her laptop, taking one of the

soft peppermint candies out of the dish sitting on the coffee table. There had been a bag of them leftover from the reception, and she had poured some out into a little holly-painted China bowl from the set Rhonda had given her, along with a steaming mug of hot cocoa. She knew she still had some Christmas gifts to wrap, but she couldn't stop thinking about her upcoming honeymoon, and she wanted to explore what else they might be able to do on their trip.

The treehouse hotel that she had booked for their honeymoon was by far her favorite part of the entire vacation. She'd always wanted to stay in one like it, and Spencer had gamely agreed, even though she thought he might actually be more comfortable in a more luxurious, traditional hotel. But he had told her that he'd married someone adventurous, and he was looking forward to finding out if it would rub off.

The treehouse itself did have a few creature comforts—from a huge clawfoot copper tub near a big window overlooking the view, to a small kitchen with all of the things they would need to cook if they didn't want to go out to eat. It was glamorous and rustic all at once, and Margo felt a shiver of excitement every time she thought about embarking on a new experience with the person she loved most in the world.

She flicked through pictures of other trips, photos from articles and magazine spreads, her excitement growing with each passing minute. They were leaving after the New Year, and while she'd grown accustomed to spending her winters firmly in the cold, she was excited for the tropical destination. She'd spent plenty of Christmases in places that were warm and balmy, and while the snow had grown on her, she had to admit she liked wearing shorts in January.

Looking around the living room again as she reached for her mug of hot cocoa, she felt a warm sense of belonging, mingled with the excitement for an adventure in a way that felt more satisfying than she could ever have imagined. It had only been a few short days since their wedding, but she already felt at home in the little house they now shared, as comfortable as if it had always been hers.

Spencer was right, she reflected, glancing back at her laptop screen. Home was wherever the people that they loved were.

She heard the door open, and the sound of Spencer kicking snow off and shrugging out of his coat. A moment later, she saw him walk into the living room out of the corner of her eye, and he dropped down onto the couch next to her, letting out a tired sigh.

"What are you up to?" he asked, and Margo smiled, setting her laptop aside.

"Just daydreaming about our honeymoon. I should be finishing up with the gifts that need to be wrapped," she admitted wryly. "But I'm so excited. I can't stop looking at our itinerary."

"Tell me about it again. I'm going to make myself some cocoa." Spencer stood up, going to get his own mug of hot chocolate, and came back, some of Rhonda's homemade marshmallows piled on top. He grabbed one of the peppermint candies, popping it into his mouth as he relaxed back against the couch next to Margo. "Tell me all about our honeymoon plans."

Margo smiled, happy with how quickly he wanted to indulge her excitement—and how excited he was, as well. "You already know about the treehouse," she said, and Spencer nodded.

"Yes, a week living among the birds and monkeys. A wild experience." He smirked, and Margo swatted him on the arm.

"I hope we get to see some. We're going on an excursion to see the penguins."

"That, I am really excited for." He smiled. "I

know you'll take tons of photos, but we should especially get pictures of that. The kids will love seeing them. And all of the wildlife, really."

"There are lots of wildlife tours," Margo said. "Giant tortoises, Komodo dragons, and we have a snorkeling trip too."

"Snorkeling in January. That does sound divine," Spencer agreed.

"Right? Warm weather and bathing suits. I can't wait." She took another sip of her hot cocoa. "And we have an excursion to see the volcanoes. The lava tunnels—"

"Tunnels?" Spencer raised an eyebrow, and Margo laughed.

"It's perfectly safe, I promise."

"I imagine you're looking forward to all of the hiking. And the photo opportunities." He smiled. "I'm going to come home in better shape than I've been in my entire life."

"I'm most excited to take pictures of us," Margo said softly. "Our first vacation photos, us embarking on our married life together. The adventure that I'm looking forward to most of all."

"We haven't really talked about what that looks like much," Spencer said thoughtfully, taking another sip of his cocoa. "The wedding and

honeymoon planning has been such a whirlwind.
We haven't really discussed our day-to-day when we
get back."

"Well..." Margo considered. "I mean, some
things won't really change all that much. You'll still
be working at the clinic, and I'll still be working at
The Gazette and teaching my photography class on
Saturday mornings. Our routine won't be much
different."

"Speaking of the clinic," Spencer added, "I met
with Aiden today. After we get back from our
honeymoon, he's going to start on an expansion to the
building. With the influx of new patients, we could
really use the space. I think it will be a good thing for
everyone."

"That sounds wonderful," Margo smiled. "What
about the rest of it? Do you want me to start having
dinner ready for you every night?" she teased, and
Spencer laughed.

"Absolutely not. In fact, I've been thinking about
hiring a second doctor to add to the practice."

"So you can come home and cook *me* dinner?"
Margo laughed as well, and Spencer grinned.

"Honestly, it's because of Caroline. I think I've
tended to handle everything as a one-man operation
for a long time, with just the receptionist and two

nurses because they're necessary. But with this new patient load, I think it might be time to have a second set of hands on the wheel. I was resistant to the thought at first, just as I think your sister was. As laid-back as I can be, the clinic is a part of my family, and I liked having it all under my control. But..."

He trailed off for a moment, looking at Margo fondly over the rim of his mug.

"I've seen how much having Shelby there has freed up her time," he continued. "She's mentioned getting to spend more time with Rhett and the kids because of it. And now that we're married, I want to soak up every second with you. If we get a dog, or have kids, I want to enjoy all those moments too. You made this place your home again to be with me, and I want to go on adventures with you. For that, I need more time. And a second member of the practice will give me exactly that."

Margo leaned forward and kissed him, happiness flooding her. "I love this," she said softly. "Your adventurous spirit taking off, as I'm getting used to the idea of having a solid home. We're meeting in the middle, a team, just as we should be. And now I have the thing I never had in my wandering days: a solid home base to come back to, a place I'll always want to call home." She smiled, leaning into him as she reached for a peppermint candy and popped it into his mouth. "We're the perfect team, Spencer. And I love it so much."

"Life should always have balance," Spencer agreed. "And I think going away with you for a little while will make returning home even sweeter. We can have both. Adventure and home, together."

"And I'll always feel at home, wherever we are, because I'm with you," Margo added, spinning her ring around her finger with her thumb. "But here, most of all."

Spencer set his mug aside, sliding an arm around her as he kissed the top of her head, and Margo laid her head on his shoulder. Just then, the house felt more like home than ever, with the tree twinkling merrily with their combined ornaments—his assortment of family ornaments and hers that she had collected from various countries over the years—and the fire crackling merrily across the room from them. She let out a long breath, feeling herself relax, unwind, safe and comfortable in a way that she only felt here, with him.

"Evergreen Hollow is our home base," he said, his arm wrapped tightly around her. "And it always will be. But I want you to know that I'll also always be up for an adventure with you."

Margo's heart warmed at that, and she looked up, a smile spreading across her face as she leaned up to kiss her new husband once more.

"Every day here with you feels like an adventure," she said softly. "No matter where we are."

CHAPTER TWENTY-THREE

It was Caroline's first year getting *two* children ready for Christmas at The Mistletoe Inn, but thanks to all of Shelby's help, it had been so much easier and more enjoyable than she could possibly have expected.

Since the wedding, Shelby had continued to show Caroline every day that hiring her really had been the best decision. She was always prompt in the mornings, ready to help with the breakfast service, eager to do whatever little tasks she could take off of Caroline's hands. And Caroline had gradually become more and more comfortable taking long lunches with her children, and heading home at five, assured that the social hour for guests was in good hands.

She'd told Shelby that she would be at the inn more often once Jay was back in school, especially around lunchtime, but Shelby had waved her off and told her to make her own hours and not feel guilty about it. It was the perk of running your own business, after all.

Caroline had never really let herself accept that until now, but more and more, she felt as if she were able to let go by degrees, actually enjoying her time away and soaking up all of the little moments that she was able to. And she'd never appreciated it more than on Christmas Day, as she flitted back and forth between the inn and her cottage.

Rhett had the day off from the fire station, unless there was an emergency, and he'd pitched in too. Caroline had gotten up early that morning to make fresh, hot cinnamon rolls for herself, Rhett, and Jay, complete with hot cocoa and the marshmallows that her mother had finally managed to teach her to make from scratch.

She'd headed over to the inn afterward, confident that Shelby would have handled breakfast for the few guests who were staying over Christmas, and helped prep the lunch for a couple who had purchased the full meal plan in their reservation, then assisted Rhonda with getting started on

Christmas dinner. Shelby had pitched in with that too, and while not all that long ago Caroline would have thought it would feel like an intrusion, now it felt like having a close friend there to join in on the delight and joy of the day.

Around lunchtime, she went home to make mozzarella chicken melt sandwiches and tomato soup for lunch, and start getting everyone ready for Christmas dinner. Rhett dressed up in a pair of dark gray chinos and a forest green shawl-collared sweater with little wooden toggles on the front, a birthday present from Rhonda earlier that year.

Caroline forewent her jeans and flannels, one of only a few times during the year that happened, instead opting for a festive red sweater dress, with a pair of tall black boots. Jay had a handsome red and green checkered button down with his own pair of chinos like his father, and they bundled Toby into an adorable pair of sweatpants with a sweater embroidered with gingerbread men. She gathered up a tote bag stuffed with the remaining few presents that she needed to put under the tree and surveyed her small family, all eager for the holiday festivities.

She had always loved routine, and tradition, and structure. It was one of the things she loved about the holidays, for all their chaos, there were the same things that they did as a family every year, moments she could rely on, and look forward to. And now, she reflected as they headed up the hill to the inn, she was getting to enjoy those traditions even more because she'd relaxed her expectations a little, and agreed to have Shelby come on to help.

This Christmas was even more full of special moments with her family, because she'd gotten to relax and enjoy them more. And she would keep that in mind, going into the next year, to keep from falling back into those old habits.

As they walked into the back door of the inn, she was hit with the familiar smells of sweet frosted sugar cookies, rich fudge, and the scent of a cooking roast with vegetables being braised along with it.

Rhonda was in the kitchen, a glass of wine at her elbow that she took sips from as she got down the China from the cupboard, puttering around and finalizing the last things that needed to be done for the evening. As Caroline carried Toby into the living room to hand him over to her father, who she knew would want to hold him for a little while until the other grandchildren arrived, she smiled at the sight of the living room all decked out.

The tree was glowing softly by the largest of the windows, the fir garlands strung along the mantle and staircase, and over the door, The fire was crackling, and all the stockings were hung up, full of the candy and small gifts that would be distributed later.

Caroline tucked the last few presents that she had wrapped that afternoon under the tree, heading back into the kitchen to help Rhonda as Rhett and Jay relaxed in the living room, Rhett already chatting with Donovan about the next year's hunting season. There would be a Christmas dessert board later, and Caroline always liked helping her mother arrange it.

Just as they were finishing up the last touches on dinner, Caroline heard the sound of the door opening, and familiar voices as the rest of the family started to arrive.

Nora and Aiden were the first to get there, Madison's happy cooing echoing through the house, a moment before a flurry of barking and skittering paws announced that Chessie had come along as well.

Caroline walked out to see Aiden and Nora both wearing Christmas sweaters—hers with bells and snowflakes embroidered on the front, his with pine trees—and Madison wearing a red and white striped candy cane sweater. Chessie, who was running in circles around their feet, was wearing a matching sweater, her ears dragging along the floor as she took off toward the warmth of the fireplace.

"Looks like you already have the puppy thing down," Caroline remarked with a laugh as Nora closed the door, carrying Madison over to join Toby. "Right down to the matching clothing."

Nora laughed too, tucking a piece of dark hair behind her ear as she handed Madison over to Donovan and went to join Caroline, Aiden sitting down next to Rhett. "We're getting there," she said with some amusement. "One day at a time."

"Come help me start setting the table?" Caroline asked. "Margo and Spencer should be here soon."

A little while later, just as Caroline and Nora were finishing up the table settings and lighting the candles, the sound of Spencer and Margo arriving was announced with another flurry of barking from Chessie. Margo walked in a minute later, wearing a red tartan jumpsuit with a green belt, her hair in looped milkmaid braids around her head, her camera bag in her hand. "Anything I can help with?" she asked, and Rhonda motioned for her to come and help start taking dishes of food out to the table.

The inn was bursting at the seams with

Christmas merriment, it felt like to Caroline. She could hear the happy sounds of Jay, Madison, and Toby playing in the living room, Jay watching over the two babies like a good older brother and cousin. There was the hum of the men talking in the living room, and the happy yips from Chessie as she got petted and scratched by the various family members sitting around the living room. Spencer came into the kitchen to ask if he could help as well, not long after he and Margo arrived, as if he already missed being near her. It was abundantly clear, just looking at the two of them, that they were blissfully happy as newlyweds.

"Our first Christmas married," Margo sighed happily as the family all sat down to eat, briefly resting her head on Spencer's shoulder before reaching to pour them glasses of wine. "It's the best Christmas yet."

"Tell us about the honeymoon you've planned," Rhonda urged, as Donovan began to carve the pot roast and she passed the dishes of sides down the table. "It sounds like a thrilling adventure."

"Very much so," Spencer said with a smile. "And lots of hiking."

"Margo's favorite," Nora said with a laugh, and Margo grinned.

"But I'm looking forward to visiting a new place," he continued, reaching over to squeeze Margo's hand, his wedding band glinting in the candlelight. "This means a lot to both of us—me trying new things, and Margo sharing with me what she loves. I'm excited to see all of it. Especially the penguins," he added, and Jay let out an excited yell.

"*Penguins?*" He bounced in his chair, leaning forward to look at Margo. "And lots of other animals too, right?"

"Lots of them," Margo confirmed. "Tortoises and Komodo dragons and sharks. And I'll have a waterproof camera with me as well, so I can take pictures of all of it."

Jay was beside himself with excitement over that prospect, and the rest of the family also couldn't wait to see the photos and souvenirs that Margo would bring back.

"I've always wanted to travel more," Shelby said, from her seat between Rhonda and Caroline. She had come back just before dinner, wearing a pretty navy blue sweater dress, invited to come and share the family meal by both Rhonda and Caroline, and encouraged by everyone else as well. She'd decided to split her evening between their family and Audrey's, and would be heading back over there for dessert and presents. "Maybe hearing your adventures will be just the push I need to do more of that."

"I hope so," Margo said. "I would love nothing more than to be the reason you went on more adventures. You should come to my wildlife photography class," she offered. "Maybe sit in and audit a session, and then sign up, if you'd like."

"I'll do that," Shelby said with a smile, as the last of the dishes were passed around and the family began to dig in to their Christmas meal.

"I'm glad you're here with us for dinner," Caroline said, glancing over at her as they all began to eat. "You've played a big role in helping Christmas happen the way it always has, by being here to be an extra set of hands. Goodness knows we needed them, with all of the wedding planning, and then Margo sending us all on a wild goose chase for her rings that were in the spice cabinet all along." She looked at Margo teasingly as she said it, and Margo threw up her hands, grinning good-naturedly.

"I'm never going to hear the end of that, am I?"

"Every Christmas," Caroline promised, and everyone laughed.

After dinner, everyone said their goodbyes to

Shelby as she headed back to Audrey's for dessert, and gathered in the living room to open gifts. Before long, there was a sea of wrapping paper strewn around the living room, and just as Caroline and Nora went to start gathering it up, Chessie broke loose from Aiden's arms, tearing through it. A flurry of wrapping paper escaped the space near the Christmas tree, flying everywhere as Chessie, wrapped in it, began barking and running wildly in circles, sending bits of paper all around.

"Oh my." Nora covered her face with her hands, but Caroline just laughed, going to scoop up the wayward dog and bring her back, as she brushed the remnants of wrapper off of her.

"We'll get it cleaned up," Caroline said with a smile. "But that's hardly the priority right now, right?"

Nora raised an eyebrow. "Is that my older sister saying that?"

Caroline laughed. "I've learned to loosen up a bit," she said, holding the puppy as Jay noisily unwrapped his new video game. "And it's done me more good than I could have imagined."

With a living room full of family, and three kids, it was noisy and chaotic, she thought. But it was also warm, and sweet, and full of happiness, full of memories of past years and the ones they were making right then, and all of the ones they would make in the future.

It was, Caroline thought, everything that Christmas should be.

There was a new tradition in the Stoker household—
one that they'd started three years ago, the Christmas
after Margo and Spencer had gotten married. With
all of the grandchildren that had become a part of the
family, Rhonda had had the idea of going Christmas
Eve caroling that year.

It had been a wonderful time, with other
neighbors joining in until there was a huge group
going from house to house, and it had been declared
a success later, over mugs of eggnog and hot cocoa.
And so, a new Stoker tradition had been born.

Now, they were all bundled up in their
Christmas sweaters, hats and scarves, gloves and
boots, getting ready to go out.

Nora couldn't help thinking, looking at them all, how much everyone had grown.

Madison was five, walking along with everyone else in her furry-collared coat and snow boots, her cheeks pink from the cold. Toby was toddling along next to her, wearing a mini Carhartt-style coat similar to the one his grandfather always wore. Jay was a teenager now, and ever the good big brother, making sure to help the kids stay nearby, and holding Chessie—who was a full-grown dog now, out along with the rest of the family in her sweater and booties —on her leash as they walked.

And there was a new addition too, one that made Nora smile so widely her face hurt every time she thought of it. Margo was standing along with everyone else, holding her new daughter Lila, who was looking wide-eyed at all of the houses covered in Christmas lights, with all of the wonder of a child experiencing her first Christmas.

Of the three of them, Margo was the one Nora would have thought the least likely to want kids, but she had been over the moon last year when she'd found out she was pregnant. And now, she was glowing with happiness as she stood next to Spencer, pointing out the snowmen and reindeer to her daughter.

"I'm cold," Toby said a little while later, as they made the last of their rounds to the houses, singing *Silent Night* at the end of their route. "I can't feel my nose," he added, announcing it loudly, making the adults all laugh.

"Well, we have hot chocolate and homemade marshmallows waiting back at your house," Rhonda informed him. "Your mother and I got it all ready before we left. So how about we head back there, hmm?"

"Good idea," he agreed, and Rhett chuckled as he took his son's hand, the group turning to head back to The Mistletoe Inn, and Caroline and Rhett's small cottage further back on the property.

Once there, they all trooped inside, knocking off the snow and piling out of boots and coats and cold-weather accessories. There was a pile of it all by the time everyone had gotten down to their actual clothes, and Caroline and Rhonda headed to the kitchen to start gathering up hot drinks and cookies, as Margo put *Miracle on 34th Street* on for the kids to watch. All of the cousins piled onto the floor, where throw pillows and blankets were spread out in front of the fire, eager to watch the movie in the warm coziness of the cottage with the fireplace flickering nearby.

Nora hung back, watching them all, feeling a warm happiness that she had grown to associate with being here with her family for the holidays. Every year, something else wonderful happened, something to remind her that being here, living here, was the best choice she had ever made.

And she had some exciting news for *this* year too. She just hadn't decided when she should share it with Aiden, yet.

She was standing near the doorway, watching as little Lila fell asleep in Donovan's arms in the recliner, Chessie curled up in a ball near the fireplace snoozing as well. She could hear the clinking of mugs from the kitchen as Rhonda and Caroline started to carry out drinks and cookies, and she started to go and help, when she felt Aiden slip his arm around her waist.

"Are you all right?" he asked, leaning in to give her a quick kiss. "It's a good night, isn't it?"

"It's a perfect night," she assured him. "And I'm fine. I just—" She bit her lip. "I have your first Christmas present for you."

Aiden raised an eyebrow. She saw the wooden watch that she'd gotten him a few years ago on his wrist, one of his favorite gifts he'd ever received, he'd said. But she was pretty sure this one would top it. "Oh?" he asked with interest, and Nora nodded nervously, leaning down to reach into her purse.

"Here," she said softly, holding out the gift between them. She saw Aiden blink, taking a moment to be sure of what he was seeing.

It was a positive pregnancy test.

He looked up at her, a smile spreading across his face. "Really?" he asked, joy already filling his voice, and Nora nodded, feeling momentarily choked up.

"This is the best Christmas present," he said, pulling her into his arms. "You'll never top this one."

"That's what you said last year," Nora said with a smile, her eyes misty. "You never know."

"If I'd known you were in the mood to switch up our routine again, I would have bought you a Christmas puppy." Aiden grinned, his face full of joyful mischief.

"It's not too late." Nora laughed. "You can still do that too."

He pulled her closer at that, kissing her under the sprig of mistletoe hanging above the door, and Nora felt a wave of happiness as she melted into him. This Christmas was perfect.

But then again, they all had been—ever since she'd come home to Evergreen Hollow.

* * *

Thank you so much for reading the *Evergreen Hollow Christmas* series!

Still in the holiday mood? Then you'll love *The Christmas Lodge*! And if you're looking for more uplifting women's fiction, dive into the *Marigold Island* series!

ALSO BY FIONA BAKER

The Marigold Island Series

The Beachside Inn

Beachside Beginnings

Beachside Promises

Beachside Secrets

Beachside Memories

Beachside Weddings

Beachside Holidays

Beachside Treasures

The Sea Breeze Cove Series

The House by the Shore

A Season of Second Chances

A Secret in the Tides

The Promise of Forever

A Haven in the Cove

The Blessing of Tomorrow

A Memory of Moonlight

The Saltwater Sunsets Series

Whale Harbor Dreams

Whale Harbor Sisters

Whale Harbor Reunions

Whale Harbor Horizons

Whale Harbor Vows

Whale Harbor Blooms

Whale Harbor Adventures

Whale Harbor Blessings

Evergreen Hollow Christmas

The Inn at Evergreen Hollow

Snowflakes and Surprises

A Christmas to Remember

Mistletoe and Memories

A Season of Magic

The Snowy Pine Ridge Series

The Christmas Lodge

Sweet Christmas Wish

Second Chance Christmas

Christmas at the Guest House

A Cozy Christmas Escape

The Christmas Reunion

For a full list of my books and series, visit my website at www.fionabakerauthor.com!

ABOUT THE AUTHOR

Fiona writes sweet, feel-good contemporary women's fiction and family sagas with a bit of romance.

She hopes her characters will start to feel like old friends as you follow them on their journeys of love, family, friendship, and new beginnings. Her heartwarming storylines and charming small-town beach settings are a particular favorite of readers.

When she's not writing, she loves eating good meals with friends, trying out new recipes, and finding the perfect glass of wine to pair them with. She lives on the East Coast with her husband and their two trouble-making dogs.

Follow her on her website, Facebook, or Bookbub.

Sign up to receive her newsletter, where you'll get free books, exclusive bonus content, and info on her new releases and sales!

Made in the USA
Las Vegas, NV
16 November 2024